Mrs. Meeker's Money

Mrs. Meeker was not *a* Mrs. Meeker but *the* Mrs. Meeker, seventy-nine and worth about $30,000,000. She'd managed to hold onto most of it, too, until she hired a private detective to trace the grandson of a former lover. Several months and some $50,000 later, she realized she was being swindled and called on Postal Inspector David Madden for help. Neither one suspected that fraud was soon to be mixed with murder!

Scene: Connecticut

This novel was serialized by the Chicago Tribune Syndicate.

Mrs. Meeker's Money

by Doris Miles Disney

DOUBLEDAY & COMPANY, Inc., Garden City, New York

All of the characters in this book
are fictitious, and any resemblance
to actual persons, living or dead,
is purely coincidental.

I am very grateful to

Inspector Thomas F. Peckenham

of Hartford, Connecticut, for the interest he has taken in this book and the many helpful suggestions he has made. It is my hope that Inspector Madden somewhat measures up to the high standard of the Postal Inspection Service that Inspector Peckenham exemplifies.

Doris Miles Disney

Mrs. Meeker's Money

Chapter One

"IT'S outrageous," Ada Meeker (Mrs. Ulysses S. Meeker) said. "The most outrageous thing I ever heard of. Call the police, Joan. The chief. I'll speak to him myself."

Joan Sheldon, Mrs. Meeker's companion-secretary, didn't have to turn to the telephone directory to look up the police-station number. In the efficiently run Meeker household police and fire departments, hospital and doctor were listed in a leather-bound notebook on Mrs. Meeker's desk. Joan dialed the police number, was connected with the chief at mention of Mrs. Meeker's name and handed the receiver to the old lady who sat beside her at the desk and could more conveniently have made the call herself.

"Thank you," Mrs. Meeker said, and then, superfluously, since everyone in Medfield, with the possible exception of babies in their bassinets, knew who Mrs. Meeker was, she said into the mouthpiece, "This is Mrs. Ulysses S. Meeker, Mr. Pauling. It's just come to my attention that I've been defrauded of a large sum of money. I want you to do something about it."

"Whatever we can," the police chief said. He spoke on a cautious note, having had previous experience with Mrs. Meeker's alarums and excursions.

"I'd like to talk to you right away about it. Will you come to the house? As you may know, I don't get out much these days."

"Yes, Mrs. Meeker. I'll be over to see you as soon as I can manage it."

"How soon will that be?"

"Well, I'm in the middle of something right now, Mrs. Meeker. I'll be free in about another half hour, I'd say."

"Half an hour?" Her tone made a concession. "I'll expect you then."

She hung up and turned to Joan. "Get the Johnston file sorted out for him. I just want the expense accounts from the hotels you checked on. There's no need to show him the whole file today."

Eight hotels had so far been checked. Accounts submitted by Henry Johnston indicated expenses of nearly six thousand dollars incurred at them. Joan separated these expense accounts from the rest.

Mrs. Peck, the housekeeper, admitted Chief Pauling some forty minutes later and took him through the spacious hall to Mrs. Meeker's sitting room in the former drawing-room wing, remodeled into sitting room, bedroom, and bath five years ago, when arthritis made the stairs too much of a chore for Mrs. Meeker's daily use.

Chief Pauling, close to retirement age after forty-two years in the Medfield Police Department, had had a long, intermittent acquaintance with Mrs. Meeker, who had never been slow to voice complaints or offer advice on the work of the department. He didn't know what to expect today.

She greeted him from an armchair near the windows. She had a short dumpling figure, a withered-apple face, and all she lacked to complete her resemblance to Queen Victoria in her later years was a widow's cap and veil.

Once upon a time Ada Meeker, then Ada Rouse, had been a snub-nosed Iowa country girl of no particular background or consequence. But that had been nearly sixty years ago.

Since 1902 she had been Mrs. Ulysses S. Meeker, wife of the founder and president of Meeker Steel Products Company destined to become Medfield's major industry, growing and prospering until Ulysses S. Meeker in 1940, at the age of seventy, with no child to pass the business on to, retired and sold his controlling interest in the company to an even bigger competitor, which made it one of its subsidiaries.

It was said in Medfield that Ulysses received in the neighborhood of ten millions from the sale and that in the last decade of his life, the booming war and postwar decade, he had, through shrewd investments, doubled, possibly tripled this sum. Aside from charitable bequests that ran to about two millions, he had left his entire estate to his wife, his will offering various suggestions for ultimate disposal of the money but no binding restraints.

Since his death Mrs. Meeker, bulwarked by Messrs. Hohlbein and Garth, her attorneys, had grown tough in resistance to onslaughts on her purse. All charitable appeals were thoroughly investigated before donations were made; income-tax deductions loomed large in their selection.

There was Meeker Park, laid out years ago on land donated by Ulysses; its soaring costs of maintenance and equipment were partially borne by his widow. There was the new wing added to Medfield Public Library. There was the Ulysses S. Meeker Memorial Scholarship Fund, grown from modest beginnings to current expenditures of between eighty and ninety thousand a year. There was the expansion program of Medfield Hospital. . . .

Mrs. Meeker, then, by virtue of her husband's money, found herself regarded as the town benefactor and, through the scholarship fund, a figure of some larger prominence in the educational field.

She was no model philanthropist, however. She was a difficult old lady to deal with, crippled by arthritis, prickly, suspicious of people's motives, generous only in spurts to individual claims upon her, sharp and alert most of the time but given, in recent years, to lapses of memory, moments of extreme sentimentality formerly alien to her, and other manifestations of approaching senility.

There was no one, since her husband's death, who loved her for herself. It is doubtful that he, wrapped up in business after the first few years of their marriage, had loved her or that she had loved him in the accepted sense of the word. Without children, without basic congeniality to bind them together, they had merely grown used to each other. Each had secretly blamed the other for their childless state.

This was Mrs. Meeker in her seventy-ninth year. Most of her contemporaries were dead. She had given up travel, once enjoyed; three years ago she had given up wintering in Florida; it was too much trouble, in view of her arthritis. Her life had mostly narrowed down to the first floor of Hilltop House, the big brick mansion, painted white, that Ulysses had built right after World War I; in the last few months it had all but narrowed down to her private suite. It was easier to have her meals served in her sitting room than to sit down, just Joan Sheldon and she, in the large formal dining room. She rarely left the house these days. She looked forward to summer and warm afternoons when she could again sit on the terrace overlooking Medfield and a distant range of Connecticut hills.

It wasn't summer when she summoned Chief Pauling. It was a sunshiny March day with a touch of spring in the air. Indeed, the calendar said that it was officially spring, but snow still lay in shady places on the grounds and Wilbur Peck, the gardener-chauffeur, had as yet done no more outdoor work than to rake up the winter's debris.

Chief Pauling returned Mrs. Meeker's greeting with the deference due her age and position, sat down in the chair she indicated, and said, "Now what seems to be the trouble, Mrs. Meeker?"

They were alone. Joan Sheldon had gone back to her office across the hall to try to catch up on Mrs. Meeker's voluminous, sadly impersonal mail.

Mrs. Meeker, a veneer of calmness imposed on the sharp, agitated note in her voice, replied, "The trouble's just what I told you on the phone, Mr. Pauling. I've been defrauded by a private detective from Hartford, a man named Henry Johnston. I hired him last summer to find someone for me. I hired him on a full-time basis and according to the reports he's been sending me every two weeks, he's been devoting his full time to the case ever since. He's been looking all over —Iowa, Texas, New Mexico, Indiana, Michigan—for this person I want found and I've been fool enough to take his reports on what he's been doing in good faith."

She gave an indignant snort. "There's no fool like an old fool, is there? I've been paying him seventy-five a day and expenses and been cheated from the start, I don't doubt."

"Seventy-five a day? Mrs. Meeker! Twenty-five—fifty at the outside for a first-rate man——"

"I know. I made the offer of seventy-five myself as an inducement to take the case. He was reluctant, you see. He said it meant losing contacts, dropping out of circulation for some unknown length of time——" She broke off, then added defensively, "I could afford it. It was my decision."

"Yes, but seventy-five——" Pauling caught her eye and subsided. She was right. She could afford it. In fact, he could think of no caprice she couldn't afford.

"His expenses have run high all along. He sends them in with his reports and I pay them by separate check. There's his car and hotel bills and meals and all kinds of tips including handouts for information and it's amounted to a lot of money. Ten cents a mile for his car—you'd be surprised how that adds up. Why, his expenses alone have run into thousands of dollars since last July. And when I think it's all lies— a pack of lies—when I think——"

Her surface calm slipped. Bright red color invaded her face. Pauling intervened. "Let's take this a step at a time, Mrs. Meeker. You hired a private detective in Hartford last summer to find someone for you. He's been working for you ever since. What have you found out that makes you think he's been cheating you on his expenses?"

"Well, I've been giving the whole thing a lot of thought lately," Mrs. Meeker began. "A couple of weeks ago I added up the checks I've sent him, salary and expenses both, and it came out far too much for the little return I've had. I thought I'd better have him run up his expense account some more and come back here to talk it all over with me. So last week I called his office in Hartford. His girl—secretary, I suppose she is—said she didn't know just where to reach him at the moment. He'd been in Hartford March 10, she said, but he was out of town again now and would I care to leave a message. I said no, I'd get in touch with him later. I wondered, though, what he was doing in Hartford when as far as I knew, he was supposed to be in Detroit at the time. Then his regular report and expense account came in the mail——"

Mrs. Meeker's withered-apple face expressed indignation. She took a deep breath and continued, "According to his report and expense account he was in Detroit March 10, the day his girl said he was in Hartford! There were meals charged to me, taxis—he didn't always use his car in cities— and hotel room and all. Cheating me!"

Her hearing seemed to be good. Chief Pauling tried to be

tactful. "Could there be a mistake in the date?" he asked. "I mean, what sounded like March 10 on the phone might have——"

Mrs. Meeker stiffened. "I still hear very well but naturally, I thought of that. Or that the girl might have made a mistake. I talked it over with Joan Sheldon, my secretary. She suggested that we pick out at random a few of his other expense accounts and call the hotels where he was supposed to be staying when he sent them in. I thought that was a good idea and had her make the calls. She'd say she was trying to locate him and ask when he last stayed at the hotel and for how long. And in every single instance, Mr. Pauling"—Mrs. Meeker shook her finger at the police chief to emphasize the point—"it turned out that he'd only spent one night at the hotel or possibly two, although he was billing me for anything from one to four weeks."

At this stage it seemed to Pauling that he was dealing with another of Mrs. Meeker's aberrations; that Henry Johnston had merely been padding his expense account, checking in at a good hotel for a night or two, then moving into a cheaper one while continuing to bill Mrs. Meeker as if no move had been made.

He glanced through the expense account the old lady thrust at him. The hotel bill clipped to it showed room charges of fifteen dollars a night for eight nights; Joan's notation showed a stay of one night at the hotel.

He suggested expense-account padding, but Mrs. Meeker would have none of it. "Not but what it would be serious enough if that were it," she said. "But it's much more serious; it's fraud all the way. Mr. Johnston has done no work on my case. The reports he's been sending me"—she rapped her knuckles disdainfully on the stack of papers beside her—"are also fraudulent."

"How do you know they are, Mrs. Meeker?"

"Well, after the first two calls Joan noticed he was actually staying at the hotels he was billing me for on the date he sent me a report. She suggested that for the rest of the calls we concentrate on dates when reports were due. Which we did. And found out he registered at each one the night before he sent in his reports and checked out the next day. So it's perfectly clear to me—as it should be to anyone with a grain of sense—that he went to these hotels just long enough to concoct a report and send it off to me. Dictated them, probably, to some public stenographer. Most hotels have them, don't they?"

"Good hotels, yes."

"Well then!" She sat back in triumph.

Pauling knitted his brows in thought. After a moment he asked, "How did you get in touch with this man Johnston in the first place? Someone recommend him to you?"

The withered-apple face took on a guarded expression. "Yes. Someone in the insurance field. Mr. Johnston does investigative work for insurance companies."

"He maintains an office in Hartford?"

"He's listed in the Hartford phone book. On Eldridge Street."

"That's a bit out of the downtown section. You've been to his office?"

"No." Mrs. Meeker's guarded expression deepened. "Too long a trip for me these days."

She said nothing more on this point. And all she said about the person Henry Johnston was supposed to locate for her was that his name was Arthur Williams and that he was the grandson of an old friend from Iowa days.

There was a silent interval. Pauling stared into the wood fire crackling on the hearth and waited for more.

"Did you ever hear of this man Johnston?" Mrs. Meeker asked finally.

"No. I've had a few dealings with private detectives in Hartford but I never heard of him. Which doesn't mean much with Hartford sixty miles away. If it were Bridgeport——" He broke off, his glance settling on the telephone. "If you wouldn't mind my putting in a toll call to Bridgeport there's a private detective there, been in the business thirty years, who might know something about Johnston."

"By all means, call him."

The police chief went to the phone. The man he called had never heard of Johnston. He had a Hartford phone book on hand, however, and looked him up.

Back in his chair Pauling said, "He's listed alphabetically as Henry Johnston, insurance investigations, but he's not in the classified section under investigators. The man I called thinks that's peculiar. Says he must confine himself to an established clientele since he's not advertising himself generally. Also, he's not listed in the directory of detective agencies. You have confidence in the person who recommended him to you?"

"Oh yes." Mrs. Meeker's tone admitted no doubt on this point.

"And yet, from what you tell me, Johnston is taking money from you under false pretenses."

"He's stealing money from me, that's what he's doing! I want him arrested and sent to prison for it." She was at her most regal, her resemblance to Queen Victoria most pronounced as she said this.

Pauling suppressed a smile. "I'm afraid I couldn't arrest him, Mrs. Meeker, even if you had him right here in this room. If he's committed a crime at all, which is open to question, he hasn't committed it within my jurisdiction." He gave it further thought. "I should think it would be a matter for the postal authorities, if anyone. He's mailed you what sound like fraudulent reports and statements from all over the country and on the basis of them you've been sending him checks through the mail. So I'd say it's something for the post-office people to handle."

The angle of Mrs. Meeker's chin told Pauling that she was going to be difficult.

He was talking nonsense about jurisdiction, she declared. She lived in Medfield, she was one of its biggest taxpayers. She'd written checks to Johnston right in this room. And her late husband——

The police chief let her run on and then once more patiently spelled out the need to consult the postal authorities. She listened at last.

"Who are they?" she asked. "You're not suggesting the postmaster here, I'm sure."

"Dunston," Pauling said. "Inspector—now, what's his name? —Madden. Yes, that's it. Medfield's in his territory and there was a case we worked on together a couple of years ago."

Mrs. Meeker reached for the phone and dialed the operator. She wanted the postal inspector's office in Dunston, she said, and then added, "Will you get it for me, please? This is Mrs. Meeker and I never can get all that rigamarole of direct dialing straight . . . Thank you."

Her call was put through. She asked to speak to Inspector Madden and was told that he wasn't in.

"When do you expect him? . . . About an hour? Well, I'll drive right in. Mrs. Ulysses S. Meeker from Medfield, tell him. I'm being robbed through the mails and I've been informed it's the job of the postal authorities to do something about it."

She hung up without giving whoever had answered the

phone a chance to say a word, and then turned to Pauling. "Inspector Madden will see me in an hour. I'll want the car." She pressed the buzzer on her desk. "And Joan to sort out the papers I should bring along for the inspector to see." She paused, her old face grim. "Henry Johnston will find out he tackled the wrong one to rob of good money when he tackled me."

Chapter Two

THE postal inspector's office in Dunston wasn't exactly overrun with imperious old ladies in mink equipped with a cane and chauffeur to assist halting progress. Mrs. Meeker's arrival created a certain discreet flurry until she was seated in Inspector Madden's office and the chauffeur given a chair in the anteroom.

She had a ten-minute wait. Then Madden and student inspector Tad Chandler came in together. She identified herself before the clerk could do so, but Madden, tall and dark, courteous with a touch of reserve, showed a deflating lack of awareness of who Mrs. Ulysses S. Meeker was. He introduced Tad Chandler, drew a chair closer to his desk for the old lady, and asked, "How can I help you, Mrs. Meeker?" while Tad settled himself in the background.

"I want you to arrest a man who's robbed me of thousands of dollars." She sat forward, her hands folded over the head of her cane. "The police chief in Medfield says I should make my complaint to you because the mails were used . . ."

She was launched on her story. Madden, letting her pour it out, not all of it clear in her indignant haste to get it told, studied her. This was a rich woman, obviously accustomed to having everything go her way, perhaps as much overwhelmed by the lack of respect implicit in what she complained of as by the loss of money it represented.

Without the stimulus of questions she ran down sooner than she otherwise would have, ending with, "The man belongs in jail and I just want you to put him there as fast as you can."

"Well . . ." Madden took his time lighting a cigarette. "Let's explore it a little further, Mrs. Meeker. Who recommended Johnston to you?"

Mrs. Meeker's enormous self-assurance wavered as it had when Chief Pauling asked her the same question. She hesitated and then said, "Someone in the insurance business. That's Mr. Johnston's field. He makes investigations for insurance companies. At least that's what he's supposed to do. But Mr. Pauling found out he's not listed in the directory of private detectives and isn't even listed in the classified section of the phone book under investigators. I'm beginning to wonder if he's not a complete fraud."

Madden's glance went to Tad Chandler, who reached for the Hartford telephone directory on a table nearby, turned the pages, and read aloud, "Henry Johnston, insurance investigations, two thirty-four Eldridge Street." A moment later he added, "No, he isn't listed in classified under investigators."

"Is there a listing under insurance? Investigators? Adjusters?" Madden asked.

Tad looked it up. "There's a listing for adjusters. No Henry Johnston, though."

"Oh. He does hide his light under a bushel."

"Because he's a crook," said Mrs. Meeker.

"And yet someone in the insurance business recommended him to you," Madden observed. "May I have his name?"

Again Mrs. Meeker showed hesitancy. She said, "I'd rather not give it to you right now. That is, I'd like to talk it over first with the person concerned. So if you don't mind——"

At this point, as his nod signified, Madden didn't mind. He asked, "What sort of impression generally did Johnston make on you, Mrs. Meeker? He must have seemed reliable and competent or you wouldn't have hired him to—— Is it a relative or friend you wanted him to locate?"

A flush touched the old lady's withered cheeks. "The grandson of an old friend. A young man named Arthur Williams. As for Mr. Johnston, I never did meet him in person. I wrote to him—Hartford's too long a drive for me nowadays —and all our arrangements were made by mail."

She saw Madden's eyebrows go up and she added quickly, "He was to have paid me a visit just before he started work on the case but he came down with a flu bug that kept him in bed for several days and in the end he called me and we just talked on the phone. He seemed to know his business from the letters he wrote and the phone talk we had. And he was so well recommended, too. I never dreamed he was a crook."

Madden leaned back in his chair, elbows on the arms, fingers steepled. He looked out the window and mentally reviewed what she had told him. She had hired Johnston last July to find a young man named Arthur Williams for her. Johnston had supposedly been working on the case full time ever since—at a very high fee—but now Mrs. Meeker had reason to believe that he hadn't been doing the job she was paying him to do and that the reports and expense accounts he sent in were fraudulent.

Embezzlement by agent, Madden thought; not a matter that came within the province of a postal inspector.

While he was formulating this thought Mrs. Meeker opened her capacious handbag and brought out an envelope stuffed with papers. Sorting them out, she handed two letters to the postal inspector. "Here's what he says, all down in black and white."

Madden looked at them before he read them. Good quality

bond paper, pica type, letterhead giving the Eldridge Street address and phone number, signature an almost illegible scrawl written with a broad-point pen, no initials at the lower left to indicate that the secretary Mrs. Meeker had mentioned had typed it, although the typing had, nonetheless, a professional look.

In the first letter, dated June 29, 1959, Henry Johnston took a negative attitude. He said that, in view of the scanty information Mrs. Meeker had on the young man she wanted found, a search for him would probably be lengthy and expensive and would require the full-time services of an investigator, to the exclusion of all his other work, for an unknown period of time. Since Johnston himself had a number of cases pending at the moment he could not quite see his way clear to undertaking such an investigation as Mrs. Meeker suggested in the immediate future.

In the second letter, dated July 3, 1959, Henry Johnston said that in view of Mrs. Meeker's generous financial offer conveyed in her letter of June 30—she must have answered Johnston's first letter the day she received it, Madden noted —he was now prepared to turn over pending cases to a colleague and begin the search for Arthur Williams the following week. In spite of the paucity of leads he hoped that he would be able to bring it to a successful conclusion.

Johnston went on to say that he felt particularly qualified to accept the case because of many years' experience in locating missing persons for insurance companies along with much other varied investigative work in the insurance field; he would, if she so desired, supply her with a number of references from local insurance companies for which he had done investigative work. He would plan to see her at her home in Medfield Monday morning, July 6, at ten, if this would suit her convenience, and suggested that she have ready for him pictures, letters, or any other material she might have that would aid in the search for Arthur Williams.

When he came to the end of the letter Madden glanced at her. "It was this appointment that Johnston's flu canceled?"

"Yes. He phoned me about it."

"Didn't he try to make another one?"

"Well, yes, he said something about it. But then it came up —I don't remember which of us mentioned it first—that the sooner he left for Somerville, Iowa, the starting point of his investigation, the better. So we talked it all over and I said I'd mail in what little information I had on Arthur Williams and a retainer. Mr. Johnston would then be in a position to start out for Iowa as soon as he felt well enough and not lose another day by coming out to see me."

"Did he supply Hartford insurance company references?"

"Well, I didn't ask for them. The fact that he was ready to supply them and had a good recommendation to begin with was enough for me." Mrs. Meeker's voice held an edge of defiance, signifying that she wasn't going to allow herself to be put on the defensive. "If he'd been able to keep his appointment with me I might have. But he was still quite sick when he called me—he could barely talk—and I didn't want to bother him with what was more or less a side issue."

A side issue. Madden said nothing. No doubt Mrs. Meeker checked very carefully the references of her household staff, people who would be under her daily supervision. But she hadn't hesitated to hire a man she had never met without asking for references; she had accepted his qualifications, vouched for only by himself and someone she knew in the insurance business, even though what she paid him was enough to staff her house twice over.

Madden felt no surprise. The inconsistencies of human nature had ceased to surprise him.

"He left for Somerville the middle of that week," Mrs. Meeker continued. "He wanted to go there first for background information on the Williamses, he said. It's the town where Arthur Williams's grandfather and I were born and raised. I didn't bring that report with me. I don't doubt but that it was honest enough, the only honest one he ever sent me. Right after that the funny business began. . . ."

Mrs. Meeker paused to extract more papers from the envelope in her handbag. "Here's his report from San Antonio the first week of August. And his expense account."

Madden read the report first. It said that Johnston had been checking newspaper libraries, motor-vehicle records, tax records, vital statistics, and so forth for information on subject's father, James Williams. Two days before the report was written he had found a record of the birth of James Williams on September 12, 1909. Johnston was now checking school records and hoped that they would yield further information.

His name was signed to the report in a neat legible hand. A small *d* under the signature indicated that it had been signed for him by whoever had typed it.

The hotel bill was the only one clipped to the expense account. It listed a room charge of fourteen dollars a night for eleven nights, telephone calls, meals, service charges, laundry; other expenses, car, cabs, tips, meals, incidentals, were itemized, the total fortnight's expenses adding up to $593.35, including expenses on the road from Iowa to Texas.

Johnston hadn't stinted himself.

"That's just one sample of his crookedness," Mrs. Meeker stated. "My secretary called the hotel. He stayed there exactly two nights, the night before and the night after he sent the report. Then he came back again for one more night when another report was due from San Antonio. It's the same thing with all the others. The pattern's too regular to say he was staying at a cheaper hotel and billing me for an expensive one. If that was the case, he wouldn't always happen to stay at the expensive hotel the one night before he was due to send in his report, would he? Why not just send it from the cheaper hotel if he was actually in the city the whole time he said he was? How would I have known the difference?"

Madden nodded. On this point Mrs. Meeker, for all her eccentricities, made sense.

He thought about fraud, as it came within the jurisdiction of the postal inspector: The devising of a scheme to obtain money or property by fraudulent representations and the use of the mails in the execution of the scheme. He went back to the letter from Hartford in which Johnston accepted the assignment and set forth his qualifications for bringing it to a successful conclusion. Rereading it, Madden decided that this wasn't, after all, a case of embezzlement by agent. Johnston wasn't yet in Mrs. Meeker's employ when he wrote the letter. If he had no legitimate standing as an investigator and hadn't been rendering the services he agreed, in the letter, to render, then he had devised a scheme to obtain money from Mrs. Meeker by fraudulent representations and had used the mails in its execution.

Madden asked, "Have you kept all of Johnston's reports and expense accounts to date?"

"Oh yes. I have a complete file of them." She implied efficiency.

"You paid him by check?"

"Every two weeks. I made out two checks, one for a thousand and fifty dollars and a separate one for his expenses."

"They run high too, don't they?" the inspector commented. "About how much money have you paid this man so far, Mrs. Meeker?"

She was silent. At last with chagrin she said, "Well, it's in the neighborhood of thirty thousand, I'm afraid."

"What bank do the checks go through?"

"A New York bank. I don't remember the name but I have all the canceled checks home. They're filed with the reports."

A New York bank for a man whose office was located in Hartford. The affair got fishier by the moment.

"I'll need to see the file," Madden said. "And have a talk with your insurance friend who recommended Johnston."

"Yes . . ." Again the hesitancy, the guardedness that mention of the recommendation brought, echoed in her voice. "Yes, of course. I'll do anything I can to help put that man in jail."

The inspector smiled. "We're a long way from that yet. In fact, before I even begin investigating Johnston the case has to be jacketed—approved, that is, and assigned a number, by the inspector in charge of division headquarters in Boston."

"Oh. How long will that take? Boston, you say? Perhaps I know someone there who——"

"That won't be necessary," Madden said firmly. "We have our own routine. I'll get in touch with you in a few days. Incidentally, if I were you, I'd send no more checks to Johnston until the picture is a little clearer."

"Indeed I won't! There's none due, anyway, until next week."

Madden asked for her address and phone number. He didn't need to write down Johnston's. They were printed on his stationery.

Madden could keep the letters, report, and expense account she had brought with her, Mrs. Meeker said. "I'll expect to hear from you in a day or two," she added, overriding the inspector's statement that it would be a bit longer than that.

She hoisted herself up on her cane. Her chauffeur came in

from the anteroom to assist her. As she took his arm she turned back. "Thank you, Inspector." Her stately bow included Tad Chandler. Then she was gone, the tapping of her cane fading out in the corridor.

"Well," said Madden. "Rather overwhelming——"

"It's being loaded with dough that does it," Tad said.

"Yes. She's rather likable in a way, though. Let's see what the Medfield postmaster has to say about her."

He went back to his desk and called the Medfield postmaster. "Joe?" he said when they were connected. "Madden here. I wonder if you can give me a little information—just a quick rundown—on a Mrs. Ulysses S. Meeker who lives in Medfield."

"A Mrs. Ulysses S. Meeker?" the postmaster repeated. "That's not the way we say it here, Dave. We say *the* Mrs. Ulysses S. Meeker, the one and only."

Madden laughed. "And you're all her loyal subjects?"

"Well, her subjects, at least. Seriously, though, from what I know of her, she's a pretty decent old girl if you don't mind kowtowing to her a bit. Her husband left her millions, God knows how many. No children, big house on the hill, Hilltop House, it's called, servants and lots of philanthropies. Park, library, hospital, scholarship fund, the whole works."

"About what I thought," Madden said. "How old is she?"

"Must be pushing on to eighty. Still pretty shrewd, though."

Not always, the inspector thought. Sentiment over the grandson of an old friend—boy friend, undoubtedly—had got in the way of shrewdness when she had paid out thirty thousand dollars to a man she had never laid eyes on. Rich as she was, a childless widow, she should have long since built a stone wall between herself and schemes to separate her from her money; but this once, at least, such a scheme had worked.

Where were her lawyers when it happened? Had she kept them in the dark?

Later that afternoon, after talking it over with Tad, explaining what made it a fraud case, Madden dictated a report on it to the inspector in charge of division headquarters in Boston.

Chapter Three

MRS. MEEKER brought her complaint to Inspector Madden on a Thursday afternoon. The weekend intervened, but by Monday morning the case had been jacketed. When the inspector had taken care of a few essentials he said to Tad, "We'll go to Hartford now and see what we can find out about Johnston."

Topcoated and hatted, they went out into the windy March day, Tad, a little taller and many years younger than the inspector, with close-cut light brown hair, eyes almost the same shade, and an intelligent, fresh-colored face. He had the general appearance of the college student he had been only three years ago, except for his conservative hat, a required article of apparel he hadn't yet accepted with resignation. Madden had a much more reserved expression on his dark scholarly face, partly innate, partly acquired through years of withholding judgment in a job where no one must be taken quickly on trust.

"I'll never get used to a hat," Tad announced as he knocked his askew getting into Madden's car.

Madden smiled. "Yes, you will. You'll come to feel undressed in public without one."

"Probably make me bald."

"I've been wearing one for years and managed to hang onto my hair. More to the point is whether your father and grandfather are bald."

"Both of them," Tad stated gloomily. "Before they reached

forty. I haven't a prayer. Better land me a wife before it happens."

Madden laughed and gave his attention to the morning traffic until they were clear of Dunston and headed for the parkway that would take them to Hartford. Then he said, "We'll go to Johnston's office first and see what kind of a setup it is."

"You expect it to be phony?"

"Well, everything else about him seems to be."

"Mrs. Meeker surprises me. You'd think she'd be too sharp to fall for his type of deal."

"Mrs. Meeker is no sharper than her arteries permit. She's nearly eighty."

"And I suppose it softened her up that when she was young she was in love with the man whose grandson she's trying to find."

"Yes. Sentimental journey into the past."

"But how gullible can you be over it?"

"I don't know," Madden said. "I don't know that there's any limit to gullibility. How many weeks ago did we have a notice from Washington that the Spanish prisoner swindle is active again? Not that it's ever really inactive."

"Be nice to have the money people have been taken for on it in the past couple of hundred years," Tad commented. "You'd think a babe in arms would dodge it by this time."

"You'd also think that the people who are persuaded to pour money into schemes to prove they're the rightful heirs to the land Trinity Church stands on in New York would look up the statute of limitations—even if they swallow the rest of the story—before they reach for their checkbooks. But they don't. In fact, some of them are mad at the post office department right now for throwing the latest perpetrators of the fraud into jail."

"Do you suppose they're passed on from father to son?" Tad inquired. ". . . And to my eldest son Horace and his heirs forever I leave the Spanish prisoner swindle complete with all the papers pertaining to it."

Madden grinned. "Couldn't be done. It's long since passed into the public domain. The only change I know of in it since its beginnings in the dim past is that it operates out of Mexico now instead of Spain."

"Basic patterns in fraud like the ten basic plots?"

"Yes. And they were probably old when Caesar was bringing Roman Law to all the Western world. Occasional new twists, of course, to bring them up to date. Nobody sells the Brooklyn Bridge these days—not that I know of, anyway —but it probably won't be long before our fraud and mailability reports begin to list sales of real estate on the moon."

Tad laughed. "The inspection service offers quite a field for the study of the gullible side of human nature."

"So it does," Madden said. "Greed and gullibility going hand in hand."

Two thirty-four Eldridge Street, a mixed business and residential neighborhood just outside the downtown area of Hartford, turned out to be the first floor of an old-fashioned house given over to small businesses, a real estate agency, an attorney and a public stenographer. Henry Johnston's name appeared on no window or door or mailbox in the vestibule. Madden headed for the public stenographer.

The lettering on her door read, "Miss Lazinski, Stenographic Service, Multigraphing, Notary Public, Typing, Mailing," and in the lower right-hand corner, "Walk In."

Madden and Tad walked into a room not much more than twelve by twelve furnished as an office with only an ornate fireplace in one wall to remind one of a different past. A woman, presumably Miss Lazinski, sat at an electric typewriter. She appeared to be in her early thirties. Not pretty, Madden thought, but displaying a nice smile that softened heavy features as she said, "May I help you?"

Madden let his gaze wander around the room, not missing the second phone on a corner table. Then he smiled back at the woman and said, "I'd like to see Mr. Johnston. Can you tell me where to reach him, Miss Lazinski?"

"Well . . ." Her tone was pleasant but noncommittal. "I'm afraid I can't. He's out of the state most of the time. This is just his mailing address. If you'd care to write to him, though, I'd be glad to forward your letter."

"You don't expect him back in the near future?"

"I really have no idea when he'll be here. But if you'd care to write to him——"

"Perhaps I'll do that, then. Thank you."

"I'm sorry I can't be more help to you." She was still smiling pleasantly as they left.

"So much for Johnston's office and secretary," Madden said when they were outside the building. "I wonder what his forwarding address is."

"She wouldn't give it to you, would she, unless you told her who you were?" Tad said.

"Too soon for that. For all I know at this stage, she could be mixed up in the affair herself."

They drove to police headquarters to see a lieutenant Madden knew in the detective bureau. He had never heard of Henry Johnston, insurance investigator. "Not that I know them all," he added. "But most of the private detectives drop in on us after they get their licenses just to let us know they're operating in our territory. No home address, you say, in the phone book?"

"Not listed, anyway."

The lieutenant stood up. "Let's see if he's in the city directory."

Henry Johnston had no listing in it.

"I don't know that an insurance investigator would have to be licensed," the lieutenant said. "Still . . ." He picked up the telephone, called the state police commissioner's office, and asked to be connected with the division of licensing private detectives and bondsmen. He had to wait for the files to be checked and then was told that no license had been issued to Henry Johnston in Hartford or elsewhere in the state.

"Just for the hell of it, I'll run an R-and-I check on him," the lieutenant said next.

Records and Identifications had no record on Henry Johnston.

"I'll try the Wheaton Detective Bureau." The lieutenant picked up the phone again. "Jim Wheaton's been a private detective for over twenty years. If Johnston's got any legitimate standing at all Wheaton will have some information on him."

Wheaton had none.

"He has a car," Madden said. "Don't know if it's a Connecticut registration."

Motor Vehicles had no car registered for Henry Johnston. He had, however, been issued a driver's license on June 12, 1959, with 234 Eldridge Street listed as his home address. Madden prompted a question as to handwriting on the application and learned that all but the signature was printed.

The lieutenant tried the Credit Rating and Better Business bureaus next. Neither one had Johnston listed.

"That's about it," the lieutenant said. "At least you know from Motor Vehicles that someone using the name of Henry Johnston exists."

"Yes. With a car registered in a different name or another

state. I suppose I'll have to get around to the insurance companies."

The lieutenant eyed him quizzically. "You're still not completely satisfied the guy's a fake? You sure dot all your *i*'s and cross all your *t*'s, Inspector."

"I can't go wrong if I stick to that," Madden said.

Tad and he had lunch before they went to the Federal Building, where their first stop was the postmaster's office, to have a cover put on Johnston's mail and arrange an interview with the letter carrier whose route included Eldridge Street. The letter carrier wasn't due back at the post office for another hour; in the meantime Madden and Tad went to the postal inspector's office on the second floor. Only one inspector was in. Madden told him that he was working on a fraud case and that one of the things he wanted to find out was when the suspect, Henry Johnston, had had a phone installed at 234 Eldridge Street. "Do you happen to have an inside contact with the telephone company?" he asked. "It would save my going through channels."

"I can probably get the information for you," the Hartford inspector said.

He made a call to the telephone company office, talked with someone he knew, and presently hung up and turned to Madden. "Johnston applied for the phone January 29, 1959, which means that he just about beat out the February 4 deadline for a listing in the new directory. There's no way to tell from their records if he's been paying his bill in cash or by check—no n.g. checks, anyway, they'd show—but he has been paying it regularly every month. No long-distance calls billed to him in the past six months, the length of time they keep the slips."

Madden glanced at Tad. "So now we know the fraud was

planned at least as far back as January 1959. Let's see what we can find out about Miss Lazinski."

The city directory supplied her first name—Gertrude—and home address. This data went down in Madden's notebook. From the telephone directory he added her home and office phone numbers. Her home phone was listed under Stanley Lazinski. The city directory gave his occupation as machinist, his wife's name as Anna. Miss Lazinski, then, was no bachelor girl with an apartment but lived at home in what was, the Hartford inspector said, a respectable middle-class neighborhood.

The credit bureau gave her an A-1 rating. The Better Business Bureau had no record of complaints on her. A call to the Municipal Building elicited the information that Stanley Lazinski owned the house he lived in and that the taxes on it were paid up to date.

A picture of Miss Lazinski as a member of a responsible, home-owning family began to emerge.

A little later the letter carrier for Eldridge Street added detail to the picture. Miss Lazinski had occupied her present office for the past nine or ten years, he said. She always had a friendly word when she saw him. Her fellow tenants spoke well of her. Her mail included nothing out of the ordinary. He had never seen anyone questionable coming or going from her office. As far as he knew, she had a successful little business of her own and was a reputable person, not likely to be mixed up in a fraudulent enterprise.

The only information he could give Madden on Henry Johnston was that he had so little mail that the letter carrier had sometimes wondered why he went to the expense of a mailing service.

When Madden told him that he had put a cover on Johnston's mail, he said, "Well, let's hope more people start writing to him."

Madden didn't think they would. Without Mrs. Meeker's checks, he thought, Henry Johnston's mail would virtually cease to exist; Johnston himself, in that identity, would soon cease to exist. But until he did, a cover on his mail would give Madden a record of any he received, the date of delivery, the postmark, and the return address if there were one.

Madden talked next with the letter carrier who delivered the Lazinski home mail. The family was well regarded, he said. It consisted of the father and mother, a Polish immigrant grandfather and several children. They kept their home in good condition, the old grandfather had a vegetable garden in the back yard and took great pride in it; the youngest girl, who was still in high school, had just won first prize in some sort of essay contest and had her picture in the paper; there was a son in college on a merit scholarship from the machine-tool factory where his father was employed.

On the way back to Dunston the inspector discussed with Tad what they had found out about Miss Lazinski. "I don't think she's involved with Johnston," he said. "I think it's all right to take her into my confidence and see what she can tell me about him. It probably won't be much but at the very least I'll find out what he looks like and what kind of an impression he made on her."

Tad gave a sigh. "You know, it scares me to think of going out on my own on a case, making up my mind on who can be trusted and all that."

"You'll make mistakes and learn to live with them," Madden said. "We all do. After a while experience cuts down the percentage. That's the most any of us can hope for."

Tad looked relieved. "No infallibility among postal inspectors?"

"No infallibility anywhere I know of this side of Heaven," Madden said.

The next morning Mrs. Meeker, expecting quick results, phoned the postal inspector. He told her that he'd just begun his investigation of Henry Johnston but what he had found out about him so far indicated that he was not a bona fide investigator.

"I told you so," she said in triumph. "I told you he was a crook."

"That's right, you did," Madden agreed. "Now, when would be the best time for me to come out and see you, Mrs. Meeker? Tomorrow morning? I want to talk the whole thing over with you and see your file on Johnston." He paused. "I also want to have a talk with the insurance man who recommended him to you."

"Well . . ." She was hedging. "I haven't got a free minute tomorrow. Then, too, before I bring names into it, I ought to have a talk with the man myself. In all fairness, I mean. And I might not be able to arrange it for another day or two."

Her evasiveness on this point puzzled Madden. He said, "A thirty-thousand-dollar fraud seems to have been perpetrated on you, Mrs. Meeker. Doesn't that make the question of fairness pretty academic?"

"Yes, I guess it does. Shall we say Friday morning at eleven?"

"That'll be fine," Madden said. "I'll see you then." As he hung up, his thin dark face still wore a puzzled look over Mrs. Meeker's reluctance to name the person who had recommended Johnston. He suspected that the recommendation hadn't been quite as glowing as she had made it sound when she first mentioned it, and that the insurance man, meeting Johnston through a casual contact, had taken him at his face value. Whatever the situation was, she would have to name the insurance man Friday. The inspector had no intention of working on the case with one hand tied behind his back.

Mrs. Meeker, her face revealing doubt and indecision, remained at her desk after she had finished talking with Madden. Presently she brightened. She'd telephone tonight and try to find out more about the recommendation from the insurance man. After all, she'd always prided herself on being fair, hadn't she? Ulysses used to call her Judge Meeker because she insisted on having all the facts before she reached a conclusion. In this case, no matter what she found out she'd have to get it all straightened out somehow before she saw the postal inspector Friday.

It occurred to her that she leaned more on other people's advice these days than she used to. Age was creeping up on her. Soon she'd be eighty. Unbelievable. Only yesterday she'd been Ada Rouse, excited about the new dress she was having made for high-school commencement. Art had sent her roses. He'd told her that she looked beautiful. Only yesterday . . .

She gave herself a shake. It wasn't only yesterday. It was 1899, nearly sixty-one years ago. Art had been forty years in his grave.

She sighed heavily. She felt old and tired. She'd have to start all over again to find Art's grandson and namesake. She'd thrown away thousands of dollars on a search for him that had never been made.

Chapter Four

"IT will be tycoonish, circa 1900," Tad predicted when they reached Medfield Friday morning and asked directions to Mrs. Meeker's.

"And what," Madden inquired, "is your idea of a tycoonish house, circa 1900?"

"Oh, gables and towers, a moat and drawbridge, for all I know. Pseudo-Gothic or whatever."

Madden followed directions through a good residential area to a better one that led to Medfield's sanctuary of wealth high on a hill.

Highest of all, Hilltop House loomed ahead surrounded by parklike formal grounds. Tad was the first to catch a glimpse of it and said, "I was wrong. The late Ulysses S. did not see himself as a feudal baron, after all."

Now Madden saw the house, white with a pillared veranda across the front, and laughed. "Not a tower in sight."

"No, it's Mount Vernonish."

A driveway turned off the road between brick gateposts painted white. "House must be brick too," Tad remarked. "Slave quarters in the rear, I suppose."

"You do the late Ulysses S. an injustice," Madden informed him. "He was a philanthropist."

The driveway took them up the last slope of the hill to a level stretch of lawn that brought the house into full view.

"I never shed tears over injustices done the rich," Tad said.

"I tell myself that somewhere along the way—hey, look at all the cars! What——"

"Police cars." Madden slowed down and found a place to park among them. Premonition told him that Mrs. Meeker would not be able to keep her appointment with him this morning.

A patrolman on duty outside came forward. Madden produced his identification folder. The patrolman looked at it and said, "Chief Pauling is here, Inspector. Maybe you'd better talk to him. If you'll wait just a minute . . ."

He left them on the long pillared veranda so like Mount Vernon's that it should have had the Potomac flowing in front of it. In no time he came back and said, "Will you go in, please? The chief will see you."

They went into the house. Chief Pauling came out of a room on their right, talking with a uniformed lieutenant who continued on along the hall. He shook hands with Madden and then with Tad when Madden introduced him.

They went into the room and sat down. "Mrs. Meeker was found dead in bed this morning by her housekeeper," Pauling began. "Her doctor called in the medical examiner.

"She was found lying flat on her back, the bedclothes drawn up neatly around her. It looked as if she'd died in her sleep at first. But when she was examined bits of blue lint and thread were found in her mouth and nostrils, changing the whole picture. Her bed linen is blue. The doctors think she may have been smothered with one of her own bed pillows. . . ."

Chief Pauling went on to say that the police had been summoned and an investigation, based on the assumption that Mrs. Meeker had not died a natural death, was now under way. Her body had been removed to Dunston General Hospital for examination. Police technicians had taken over her private suite and other officers were going through the rest of the house. Mr. and Mrs. Peck, gardener-chauffeur and housekeeper respectively, and Joan Sheldon, Mrs. Meeker's companion-secretary, were the only other permanent members of the household. In questioning them, the only point of any consequence that had come to light so far was that Joan Sheldon and Mrs. Meeker hadn't been getting along too well lately, in fact, not since last fall when Mrs. Meeker had broken up a budding romance between Joan and a local young man.

"Doesn't seem to mean too much, though," Pauling interpolated. "Fellow got married to another girl last month and Miss Sheldon's not lacking dates, I gather. I must say she made a favorable impression on me, not trying to hold back at all when she talked to me. Of course, at the beginning of an investigation it's hard to tell what matters and what doesn't. You're all over the lot."

He said next that the daily woman, who had appeared at her usual eight-thirty, seemed to have nothing to offer and had been questioned briefly and sent home; that Mrs. Meeker's lawyers had been notified and that one of them would arrive very soon.

Madden asked, "Did you get an estimate from the medical examiner on the time of death?"

Chief Pauling made a grimace. "You know how they are. At least four hours, he said, and not over eight. This was at eight this morning when he first saw her. The pathologist will bring it much closer, of course, from the stomach contents. She had dinner, broiled chicken and so forth, at seven last night and ate nothing afterward."

"Signs of forced entry?"

"None. Just a full-blown argument about an unlocked door. Mrs. Peck says she made her usual rounds at ten-thirty checking on doors and windows. Then she looked in on Mrs. Meeker who had gone to bed at ten and was sound asleep lying on her side facing the windows. She liked to have a night light left on in her sitting room and the door to her bedroom open. Mrs. Peck says there was nothing out of the way then. The house was locked up tight and Mrs. Meeker asleep when she went up to bed. Her husband had gone up ahead of her but was still awake. They talked a few minutes but were asleep by eleven and didn't hear a thing that disturbed them during the night. Then Mrs. Peck got downstairs at seven this morning and went into Mrs. Meeker's rooms. The night light was still burning in the sitting room, everything was the way she'd left it the night before except that Mrs. Meeker was dead. Mrs. Peck says she thought it was the old lady's heart or something. She called the doctor and then roused the others and told them.

"When we got here, we found the french door in the dining room unlocked. Miss Sheldon came in that way last night. Going on midnight, she says. Has her own key. She didn't try the door first because she knew Mrs. Peck made a habit of locking it. When she was inside she just closed the door which would then lock automatically. We've examined it. If she took hold of the knob to close it she could have accidentally released the catch but she says she closed the door without touching the knob. So there you are. This morning we found it unlocked."

"Which suggests several possibilities," Madden remarked. "Mrs. Peck could have missed up on locking it and someone got in before Miss Sheldon came home or later in the night; or Miss Sheldon accidentally hit the catch and released the lock when she closed the door after her; or it's a red herring, intended to make an inside job by one of the three look like an outside job; or the door wasn't the means of entry at all."

"Which still makes it a red herring," Pauling said.

"Yes. Anyway, it's a little farfetched that the one night a door was left unlocked by oversight some prowler came straight to it, and instead of getting out of the house when Mrs. Meeker heard him, smothered her with a pillow."

"I know. But we've checked all the doors and windows and none of them show signs of entry. Just that one door unlocked."

Tad said, "Isn't there still another possibility? That an outsider was given or somehow got hold of a key?"

Madden looked at him with approval. "Yes," he said.

Pauling sighed. "Gets more complicated by the minute. Nothing disarranged, nothing, so far as we can discover, missing. . . ."

The postal inspector stood up and wandered around the room eying the pictures, bric-a-brac, and general décor, seemingly unchanged since the house was built. He contemplated without admiration a large, gilt-framed picture of valley and mountain crags that was not a good example of the Hudson River school and he asked without turning his head, "Where do they all sleep?"

"Miss Sheldon has a bedroom over Mrs. Meeker's rooms; the Pecks have their quarters over the garage, which is attached to the house."

Madden teetered back and forth on his heels, still contemplating the painting. "I shouldn't call it the ideal arrangement to leave Mrs. Meeker alone on the first floor. Not considering her age and infirmities."

"That's what I thought. But she had a bell right by her bed that rang in the Pecks' rooms. And a house phone in the sitting room. And Miss Sheldon right up over her. If she needed anyone in the night——"

Madden, who was whistling softly to himself, turned and

said, "It looks as if it didn't do her much good to need some-one last night. The Pecks apparently slept like lambs. Miss Sheldon too?"

"So she says."

"It could be true, I suppose," Madden added after further thought. "If Mrs. Meeker was asleep at the time the whole thing could have been quick and quiet. A pillow pressed down on her face, the murderer's weight on top of it—given her age and physical condition, she'd have had practically no chance to make an outcry or fight back and free herself. She'd hardly be awake and aware of what was happening before it would be all over for her."

"Yes," Pauling said. "And under those circumstances, it wouldn't require too much strength. A woman could have done it."

"I'm not buying a prowler for one minute, but a moneyed section like this would attract them," Madden said. "Do you have many complaints?"

"About what you'd expect. None, though, from this house in I don't know how many years. It's never closed up any more, you see, and——" He broke off as a plain-clothes man appeared in the doorway. "Yes, Brown?"

"Can I speak to you a minute, sir?"

Chief Pauling excused himself, went out into the hall, and came back presently, wearing a satisfied look. "Sergeant Brown says he just noticed that one side of Mrs. Meeker's bed was made up nice and trim with mitered corners but on the side where she slept, the bedclothes were bunched in at the bottom. When he showed it to Mrs. Peck she said the bunched-in side wasn't her work. She's more particular than that. The bed wasn't like that last night, she said, when she turned it down for Mrs. Meeker."

"So now we have a picture of the poor old lady putting up

a struggle and kicking out the bedclothes on her side of the bed," Madden said.

"And her murderer tucking them in afterward to make it look as if the bed hadn't been disarranged at all. But an inexperienced bedmaker."

"Or someone subtle enough to make it look that way. Is Mrs. Peck a subtle sort of person?"

Pauling started to shake his head and changed the head-shake into a shrug. "How can I say? I never met the woman until this morning. She seems straightforward enough." He glanced at Tad with a smile. "See what detective work gets you into? You can't take a thing for granted."

"Inspector Madden's drilling that into me," Tad said.

"He should." Pauling continued, "The medical examiner says that if it's murder, the murderer was a little too smart, leaving Mrs. Meeker on her back, the bedclothes drawn up to make it look as if she'd died peacefully in her sleep. If she'd been found half out of bed or with her face turned into a pillow, they'd probably have assumed, at her age and all, that she'd had a stroke or a coronary and not have considered an autopsy necessary."

"I doubt that I'd have thought of all that," Madden commented.

"I don't know that I would have either." Pauling took out cigars, offered them around, and when they were refused cut the end off one and lit it with due deliberation. He eyed the inspector. "Now, what about her complaint of being defrauded? She told you, I guess, that I was the one who advised her to see you?"

"Yes, she mentioned it. And seemed to have a legitimate complaint. I've begun an investigation of it." Madden proceeded to relate what he had thus far found out about Henry Johnston.

At the end Pauling said, "He's a phony, all right. And took her for plenty, didn't he?"

"At least thirty thousand."

"It's too soon to say if I've got a murder case on my hands but if I have, it's a motive. Either Johnston himself or the insurance man who recommended him."

"Or both." After a moment's reflection the inspector added, "I'd be more inclined to think both. Not both physically involved, perhaps, but in collusion planning the murder."

Pauling nodded. "I can't stop with Johnston, though, looking for motives. Mrs. Meeker's estate will run to millions. There's the question of who inherits when money comes into a case. Her lawyers will have that information. She had no close relatives, according to the people here. Second cousins, a couple of great-nieces out in Oregon. No one at all living in this part of the country. They get something, I suppose, but from what I've always heard, the bulk of the estate goes to local charities and institutions."

"What about the Pecks and Miss Sheldon?" Madden asked.

"I should think there'd be bequests to them." Pauling stood up. "I want you to meet them. I haven't mentioned Johnston to them yet. Miss Sheldon said you were coming out at eleven and I thought I'd let the Johnston angle go until you got here."

He went out of the room and came back with a couple in late middle age. Mr. Peck, whom Madden had seen before in chauffeur's uniform, was a wiry, nervous-looking little bantam of a man with sharp questioning eyes. Mrs. Peck, comfortably well fed, an inch or two taller than her husband, appeared to be a more placid type. They said that they knew nothing about Henry Johnston; that they had never so much as heard his name mentioned until this minute. An insurance investigator? They hadn't known that Mrs. Meeker had hired one.

When Madden mentioned Arthur Williams, Mrs. Peck dredged into her memory and recalled Mrs. Meeker's speaking of him once or twice. This was months ago. He was an old sweetheart of Mrs. Meeker's, Mrs. Peck thought, but dead for many years.

The inspector directed his attention to Mr. Peck. "When you drove her to my office the other day, did she refer to her reason for seeing me?"

"All she said was, take her to the post office building in Dunston. And you talked so quiet while I was waiting in the other room for her, I couldn't make out what you were saying. Except once I heard her talking about somebody stealing money from her."

Resentment came into his voice as he added, "She never said a word about it on the way home, either. I was just her chauffeur. A servant. She wasn't the kind to tell servants her business. She drew a line and kept on her side of it."

Mrs. Peck hastened to soften this. "Now Wilbur, you know that wasn't quite the way it was. She kept her private business to herself with just about everyone. As far as that goes, we didn't tell her our business no more than she told us hers."

The line had been sharply drawn, though, just as Peck said, Madden reflected. Mrs. Peck accepted her status, but her husband carried a chip on his shoulder over the lack of democracy.

She said next, "Perhaps Miss Sheldon can tell you something about this private detective. Not that she ever mentioned him to us—Mrs. Meeker wouldn't have stood for it— but being her secretary, Miss Sheldon always knew more than we would about what was going on."

The inspector asked no questions about Mrs. Meeker's death. It was outside his province. He thanked the Pecks in dismissal.

Chapter Five

JOAN SHELDON, at least five feet seven and carrying her height well, came into the room. She wore a dark skirt and sweater. Her brown hair, lustrous and thick, was pinned up in what Madden thought of as a cone-shaped effect, although he assumed that she called it something else. She had brilliant blue eyes that were, on this occasion, very grave. She was more than pretty. She looked poised and intelligent. Out of the tail of his eye Madden saw Tad come alert as they stood up to greet her.

Pauling performed introductions. "Miss Sheldon, Postal Inspector Madden . . . Inspector Chandler."

"How do you do." There was a trace of nervousness in her voice, but it was an agreeable one nonetheless, Madden thought, voice-conscious through listening to so many in the course of his work.

Tad Chandler thought so too. Madden caught unqualified approval in the glance he turned on the girl.

They sat down. Pauling said, "I know you've gone through your position here for my benefit, Miss Sheldon, but would you mind telling the inspectors a little about it too?"

He was fatherly in his attempt to put her at ease. Madden offered a cigarette, lit it for her, and then his own. Tad brought out his pipe. Madden saw Joan Sheldon look at it and smiled to himself. Tad had very recently taken up pipe smoking. Girls, he'd informed Madden, were charmed by it. They thought it was virile.

Well, it drew Joan Sheldon's attention. Madden must grant Tad that.

Her gaze returned to Madden, flickering now and then to Tad, as she explained her role in Mrs. Meeker's life. Her mother, widowed in Joan's childhood, had been Mr. Meeker's part-time secretary. This was after he had sold his interest in the Meeker Steel Products Company. He still kept his office at the plant and went in several times a week to take care of correspondence and investment matters, employing Mrs. Sheldon until his death eight years ago. About a year later Mrs. Sheldon became ill, a last lingering illness that ate up money. When she died five years ago at the start of Joan's senior year in high school, there was very little left. Mrs. Meeker had come forward with the suggestion that Joan could live with her, make herself useful, until she was graduated. She had then sent her to Bay Path in Massachusetts, where she had taken a two-year course in secretarial science.

Joan paused. Sorting out her words, she said, "It was understood at the time that when I finished the course I would stay on with Mrs. Meeker as her companion-secretary. While I was at Bay Path, I did secretarial work and other things for her during vacations. She felt I was reliable and that she needed someone like me." Another pause. "Which she did. I took care of all kinds of things for her. Shopping, seeing people, reading to her, keeping her company generally, and quite a lot of secretarial work, too. You have no idea how much correspondence a woman in her position has to keep up. I feel that I've been earning my thirty-five dollars a week. I've also had room and board, of course."

Thirty-five dollars a week. Not exactly munificent, Madden thought, when the girl must have been at Mrs. Meeker's beck and call nearly twenty-four hours a day. Mrs. Meeker had how much? Millions, the Medfield postmaster had said.

The curious penuriousness of the rich struck Madden afresh. Then he reminded himself that Joan Sheldon had been too nearly grown and Mrs. Meeker too old when their lives became linked for Joan to have established herself in a daughter's—or rather, granddaughter's—place. Mrs. Meeker had simply needed and used her.

"When were you graduated from Bay Path, Miss Sheldon?" he asked.

"It will be four years this June."

Madden read between the lines. Joan had done Mrs. Meeker's bidding during her last year in high school, Bay Path vacations, and for almost four years since. She had earned her education. Mrs. Meeker had had the better of the bargain.

"I've always felt under deep obligation to her," Joan volunteered.

"What was to have happened when you got married? Didn't you discuss it?"

She flushed. Madden was amused by the involuntary glance she directed at Tad. "Yes, it came up. Mrs. Meeker said she hadn't many years to go. She hoped I'd see her through them and be in no hurry to get married. She was leaving me ten thousand in her will, she said; and for each year I stayed on with her after my twenty-first birthday she would add five thousand to it."

A grossly selfish way for Mrs. Meeker to have bought companionship, Madden thought. Open only to old people with money. Old people without money—but that was a digression. . . .

Pauling said, "And then last fall, Miss Sheldon, Mrs. Meeker played a part in breaking off an understanding—well, that's an old-fashioned word—but whatever you want to call it, with some young man?"

Silence from Joan for an interval.

Tad looked sour.

Finally she said, "Yes, Mrs. Meeker threw obstacles in the way. She'd find she couldn't spare me when I had a date with Steve; she'd practically freeze him out of the house when he came to see me, exaggerate all his faults . . ." She fell silent again. Then she said, "Perhaps I wasn't as interested in him, though, as I thought I was or I wouldn't have let her do it."

Tad looked less sour.

She added, "I have wanted to break away, just the same. I've made no secret of it. I've felt—well, buried in this house, elderly people the only ones I ever saw, never anyone my own age. Then, too, Mrs. Meeker has been getting harder and harder to please. Although I'll always be grateful for what she's done for me, I've felt these past months that I've given her enough of my life to repay her. I've wanted to leave. Even if she cut off my bequest, which she hinted at doing." Joan flushed again. "I didn't want to molder away waiting for it."

Her tone was troubled, a little embarrassed. Madden studied her. She was an appealing girl, seemingly honest, sensitive, surely incapable of smothering a helpless old woman with a bed pillow to secure a modest inheritance and freedom from a house not unlike a luxurious tomb.

As if sensing Madden's thought she said, "After all, I was free to leave whenever I made up my mind to. And it would have been soon." A moment later she added, "She couldn't have been murdered. It's too awful."

"No one's used the word murder yet, Miss Sheldon," Pauling reminded her calmly.

"But the police wouldn't go through all this if she'd just died in her sleep as we thought at first," she protested.

"We don't know yet what caused her death. We have to keep checking and rechecking to get the whole picture. Now, if you'll just tell us again what you did last night——"

She suppressed a sigh and began patiently, "I had a dinner date. I left about quarter-past six——"

"With a young man named John Lawson from Dunston," Pauling led her along.

"Yes. I met him last month."

"And you've had three dates with him since."

"It won't be four after you've finished questioning him about me," Joan observed with a flash of spirit. "He'll think I'm someone to stay away from, mixed up with the police. Not that it matters particularly." Her glance met Tad's briefly. "It isn't as if I'd known him very long."

"You left the house about quarter-past six," Pauling prompted her.

"And went to the Stone House in Dunston for dinner. Then we dropped in on Mr. and Mrs. Peter Smedley, friends of John's in Dunston. We left their house about eleven-thirty so I was home around twelve. John came up to the door with me but I unlocked the door myself; at least I turned the key in the lock. . . .

"I pushed the door closed when I was inside without touching the knob. Mrs. Peck has always been so utterly dependable about locking up at night that I didn't check to make sure the door was locked." She hesitated, frowning a little. "Looking back now, I must have felt it was locked from the way it closed. . . ."

She continued, "On the way upstairs I glanced into Mrs. Meeker's sitting room. The night light was on and everything seemed all right." Her blue eyes clouded. "I didn't look into her bedroom, though. I don't know if she was still alive at the time. I went on up to my room and went to bed. I slept right

through until Mrs. Peck woke me this morning and said Mrs.
Meeker was dead. If someone got in—if the door was unlocked, I didn't hear a sound. But I don't see how it could
have been. Mrs. Peck is so careful . . ." Her voice trailed
away uncertainly.

"Well, if she's so careful and you didn't touch the lock,
how do you account for the door being unlocked this morning?" Pauling inquired.

She shook her head. "I can't account for it."

This was a dead end. Madden turned the conversation to
Henry Johnston.

Pauling had put the girl on the defensive, but as she began to talk about Johnston her manner changed; she became
the competent secretary.

Mrs. Meeker had been secretive about him from the start,
she said. Joan hadn't known that there was such a person
until his reports began to come in. They were marked personal, as his letters must also have been, since Joan, who
sorted the mail, hadn't opened them. After about the second
or third report arrived Mrs. Meeker told her that Henry Johnston was a private detective she had hired to find Arthur Williams, the grandson of her old friend. The Williams name
was familiar to Joan; now and then Mrs. Meeker had mentioned the Arthur Williams she had known in her girlhood.

The next thing Joan found out about Henry Johnston was
that Mrs. Meeker wasn't paying him out of her regular checking account. This was when a statement came in from a Dunston bank and Joan took it to Mrs. Meeker unopened. Mrs.
Meeker said that she had opened a separate account for paying Johnston so that she would have available at a glance a
complete record of what he cost her. She made out his checks
herself instead of having Joan, who usually made them out,
do it for her. She instructed Joan to bring all Dunston bank

statements to her unopened. She said that the matter wasn't to be mentioned to Mr. Hohlbein if Joan had occasion, as she sometimes did, to discuss household expenses with him.

Poor old lady, judgment suspended, living in a fantasy of her vanished youth, refusing to let the light of reality in on it; not daring to let it in, Madden thought; knowing all along deep inside her that Johnston was no more than part of the fantasy; that what she sought could never be found.

All these months, Joan continued, Mrs. Meeker had offered no information on how Johnston's investigation was progressing. Until last week's outburst, when she'd had Joan telephoning hotels around the country to find out how long he'd stayed at them, she had scarcely mentioned his name. Joan, realizing that it was a touchy subject, had let it alone.

There were no hesitancies or evasions on Joan's part in relating this to Madden. It sounded like the truth to him.

He went on to insurance agents. Joan named the local men who handled all Mrs. Meeker's insurance, she said. If either of them had recommended Johnston to Mrs. Meeker, Joan had no knowledge of it.

"Did you see her last night before you went out?" the inspector asked next.

"Yes. I went in just before I left. I had on a new dress and I wanted to show it to her."

"Johnston wasn't mentioned or anything else that might have been on her mind?"

"No. Remember, we were getting along on the surface but underneath was the question of my getting another job. So she wasn't taking me into her confidence all winter any more than she had to. Last night there wasn't time to talk, anyway. She had a long-distance call from Brian Thayer. I answered it, talked to him for a minute and handed the phone to Mrs. Meeker. Then I said good-by and left."

"Brian Thayer?" This was the first Madden had heard of him.

"The administrator of the Ulysses S. Meeker Memorial Scholarship Fund, one of Mrs. Meeker's major philanthropies," Joan explained. "He's been in North Carolina for a week or more but I imagine he'll be back today. At least, he was calling from Philadelphia last night. It's going to be a shock to him to come home and hear about what's happened. Not that he and Mrs. Meeker were particularly close, but he's been administrator of the fund since it was established."

Pauling had gone out of the room for a minute or two. He came back and said to Madden, "I've sent someone to see Mrs. Meeker's insurance agents."

Madden nodded and didn't say that he planned to see them himself.

"Both been in business here for years," the police chief added. "Very good reputations."

If that was the case, then Madden knew ahead of time what they would say about Johnston: that they'd never heard of him, let alone recommended him to Mrs. Meeker.

The front door opened and closed and hurrying footsteps sounded in the hall. A moment later a man burst into the room, stopped short as his glance found Joan, and exclaimed, "My God, Joan, what a home-coming! They've just told me——"

This, Madden inferred, was Brian Thayer.

Chapter Six

HE was close to Madden's five eleven in height, their eyes almost on a level as they shook hands. Heavier in build, though, he didn't look that tall. He was neither good- nor ill-looking, possessing an assortment of features that were of no particular stamp. He was very pale at the moment. His eyes —green or hazel—had a shocked look.

He sat down. Pauling answered his swift flow of questions, allowing him time to collect himself. Finally Brian Thayer asked, "But why are there so many police here? Is it because she died without a doctor in attendance?"

No mention had been made of what had aroused the doctors' suspicion. None was made now. Pauling replied, "The doctors don't know just what caused her death, Mr. Thayer. Until they do . . ."

He left his voice fall away. Then he said, "Without going into all that until we know more about it, I wonder if you'd tell me a little bit about yourself, just for the record."

"Yes, of course. Anything I can do to help. Although what——" He broke off and in a quieter tone said that he came from Red Bank, New Jersey, held a master's degree in education from New York University, and had taken courses in business administration at the University of Connecticut. He had been teaching at Medfield High School eight years ago when Dr. Greer, the superintendent of schools at the time, had suggested him to Mrs. Meeker, who was seeking an administrator for the scholarship fund she was then setting up

in her husband's memory. Mr. Meeker, who had died a few
months earlier, had been awarding scholarships to needy orphan boys for years on a more or less random basis as they
were brought to his attention. Dr. Greer had suggested to
Mrs. Meeker that she establish a permanent scholarship fund
in her husband's memory. She had added the proviso that it
be limited to orphan boys, Mr. Meeker having been an orphan himself, a self-made man. Five hundred thousand was
the original contribution made by Mrs. Meeker to establish
the fund. She and two others were named to serve as a board
of trustees and Thayer selected as administrator. In the past
eight years she had enlarged the fund to two million dollars.

Thayer stopped at this point and interjected, "But all this
is a matter of public record, Mr. Pauling. Do you really want
to hear the rest of it?"

"Go ahead."

Thayer went on to say that the income from the fund totaled nearly eighty thousand a year. His work consisted of
processing all scholarship applications, interviewing the more
promising applicants in person, investigating their back-
grounds and narrowing down the list to about twenty or so
boys from among whom the trustees made the final selections.
The amount of the individual scholarships varied, depending
on need and other resources, but ran generally between fifteen and twenty-five hundred a year for the four years of
college. The scholarships differed from the usual pattern in
that they were paid to the recipients, who then paid their
own bills at the college of their choice. At any given time
there were between thirty and forty boys receiving scholarships, and Thayer found that his job kept him busy following
up those in college and processing new applications.

"Will Mrs. Meeker's death change the picture in any way?"
Pauling inquired.

Thayer's color had come back. His voice, precise and rather light, had steadied. He said, "Two or three years ago Mrs. Meeker told me she was making provision in her will to enlarge the fund. I don't know whether or not she did. It was never mentioned again and"—he smiled faintly—"it wasn't a subject I could, with grace, pursue."

Madden inserted a question. "As the fund now stands, is it an irrevocable trust?"

Thayer shook his head. "Discretionary. But she took so much interest in it, I would say the only point to consider is whether she enlarged it or not. I hope so. I can't think of a more worth-while project. But then, of course"—a self-deprecatory gesture—"it's my field and I'm not without bias."

Pauling asked, "Where is your office, Mr. Thayer?"

"In my apartment. There's an extra room I use. And I have a part-time secretary who comes in when I need her."

"Are you married?"

"Well, I was. Years ago before I came to Medfield. It didn't last long. We were divorced."

"Would you mind telling me the grounds?"

"Not at all. Incompatibility. The old saying—we agreed to disagree. My wife liked a good time, I liked to stay home and read and study. She's remarried since, I might add, and the last I heard was living in South America."

His tone was matter-of-fact, indicating no regrets, no ache of loss, no jealousy of his successor. Madden, whose own happy marriage had ended in the death of his wife, and who had never quite reconciled himself to her loss, wondered, as he often did, at the casual attitude some people seemed to take toward a broken marriage.

For the moment Pauling had no more questions about Thayer's background. He continued, "You've been in North Carolina, Miss Sheldon said."

"Yes. We have students on Meeker scholarships at Chapel Hill and Duke. We have another one at the University of Virginia so I also made an overnight stop in Charlottesville. And still another at Georgetown."

"Oh. How did you travel?"

"I had my car. I use it quite a bit on trips. I don't like flying or being tied to train schedules." Thayer's face took on a wry expression. "I suppose this is to establish my where-abouts last night, Mr. Pauling? Well, I got into Philadelphia around five-thirty and checked in at the Putnam Hotel on Chestnut Street, intending to see someone at Temple this morning. I phoned Mrs. Meeker from my room—reporting back, as it were—to tell her I'd be home sometime today."

"What time did you call her?"

"Oh, perhaps a little after six. I didn't notice particularly. Joan—Miss Sheldon—answered the phone and we talked a minute and then she gave the phone to Mrs. Meeker who immediately started telling me about being defrauded by a private detective she'd hired, a man named Johnston. She said she'd gone to a postal inspector about him." Thayer's glance strayed to David Madden. "You, Inspector?"

"Yes."

"Well then, you know about what she told me. I tried to quiet her down. She got so excited she was almost incoherent. She wanted me to come home last night. I was dead, though. I felt as if I'd take root at the wheel if I got behind it again. I hadn't had dinner yet, either. I told her there'd be no point in it. By the time I ate and got started it would bring it to midnight before I got here. So then she asked me to drive up early this morning. I didn't know what good it would do; she knew how opposed I'd been to her hiring this Johnston, and she'd already placed her complaint in the inspector's hands, but as long as she wanted another ear to pour her troubles into, I said I would come. Which I did. And walked into this. The last thing in the world——" He broke off, his headshake eloquent of disbelief.

"What time did you check out of the Putnam this morning?" Pauling asked.

"Perhaps a little before seven. I got down to the coffee shop for breakfast not much after six. I'd forgotten to call the hotel garage to have my car brought around so I stopped at the desk when I'd eaten and took care of it. Then I went up to my room, packed and checked out. I didn't look at the time but it was probably close to seven. I drove straight through, stopped at my apartment to drop off my luggage and freshen up and then came on here."

When Pauling offered no comment on this, Madden took over. "Did you ever meet Johnston?"

"No."

"What did Mrs. Meeker tell you about him?"

"You know it was the grandson of the old friend she wanted found?"

"Yes."

"The first I heard of it was early last summer," Thayer said. "I came to see her about something else and she started telling me an insurance friend—she didn't say who it was—had recommended Johnston and she was thinking of hiring him to find Arthur Williams." Thayer's precise voice took on a rueful note. "I made the mistake of opposing the whole thing and that made her more determined than ever to go ahead with it. She liked having her own way."

Here was another blank wall on the insurance man who had recommended Johnston. Madden asked, "Did you have any particular reason for being opposed to the plan, Mr. Thayer?"

"I didn't see how it could come to anything. Mrs. Meeker,

from what she told me, didn't have enough information on Williams for Johnston or any other private detective to find him. All she knew was that he was supposed to be in Texas. I felt she'd be throwing away her money for nothing."

The inspector reflected that Brian Thayer had shown unwarranted concern over what Mrs. Meeker, who was in a position to indulge her every whim, did with her money. Perhaps she had felt the same way at the time, since she had, Thayer continued, dropped the subject, telling him that her mind was made up.

"And of course it came to nothing just as I predicted," he said next. "I don't doubt but that the money she threw away on it would have put several boys through college."

So that was where the shoe pinched, Madden thought.

Thayer went on to say that Mrs. Meeker, probably because he had disapproved of her project, had said very little to him about it all these months. He had asked her now and then how the search was going, but all she would say was that Johnston hoped to find him soon, that he was following up a good lead in Texas or Indiana or New Mexico or somewhere.

She had never said so to Thayer, but he had assumed that in her youth she had been in love with the man whose grandson she wanted found.

"Old people tend to view the past through rose-colored glasses," Madden remarked.

"Yes." Thayer smiled. "I imagine she'd have been very much disillusioned if she'd ever found Arthur Williams. He couldn't possibly have measured up to her memory of his grandfather."

" 'It's to dream of, not to find'?" Madden suggested.

"Exactly. An expensive dream, too, I gathered."

There was Thayer's preoccupation with Mrs. Meeker's spending of her money cropping up again. The Johnston fraud would, of course, have financed several scholarships. But it was still none of Thayer's business.

"Was she right about being defrauded?" Thayer asked.

"It seems so."

"Then Johnston will have to return the money, won't he?"

"First he has to be caught," Pauling inserted.

But Thayer, like Joan Sheldon and the Pecks, shook his head. He had no idea, he said, who the person calling himself Johnston really was, what he looked like, where he could be found.

Mr. Hohlbein, of Hohlbein and Garth, Mrs. Meeker's lawyers, arrived and did more than shake his snow-white head over Henry Johnston. He sputtered with indignation when the question came up. Mrs. Meeker had never so much as mentioned the man to him and had never mentioned Arthur Williams, either. He couldn't understand it. Why, working on her income-tax declaration, he'd seen her quite often lately and yet she hadn't said a word about Johnston. And certainly, her checking account showed no—— A Dunston account? Mr. Hohlbein turned a color that threatened a stroke over Mrs. Meeker's having gone behind his back in this manner.

"But didn't her Medfield checking account show a withdrawal of the funds she deposited in Dunston?" Pauling inquired. "From what Inspector Madden tells me, it was at least thirty thousand."

"She kept plenty of cash in a safe-deposit box." Mr. Hohlbein's expression deplored this crotchet of his late client. "God knows how much. She would never say. But at least a million, I think. When I tried to get her to put the money to work for her—tax-exempt bonds, for example—she said she preferred having cash where she could put her hands on it at a moment's notice. In case of another crash. You couldn't change her mind on it. On anything," the elderly lawyer added as an afterthought.

He asked to see the Johnston file. Pauling said that he could see it later; that he hadn't had time to look at it yet himself. He glanced at Madden. "I'll turn it over to the inspector in another day or two. The fraud is his department."

They went on to Mrs. Meeker's will. Mr. Hohlbein said that a copy of it would be available at his office. It contained numerous personal bequests, none of them particularly large. The residue of the estate was left to various civic and charitable organizations.

Madden could see no profit in remaining longer. Tad seemed less ready to leave; but his reluctance, Madden felt, was based less on the pleasure of Mr. Hohlbein's company than on the fact that Joan Sheldon was still in the room.

Just before they left Pauling took Madden aside to tell him that Mrs. Meeker's insurance agents had been questioned and said that they hadn't recommended Johnston to her, had never heard of him as an insurance investigator or in any other capacity.

"Which is about what I expected," Madden told Tad as they drove away from the house. "Johnston's cover isn't going to be that easy to break." He added, "She said someone she knew in the insurance business."

"Yes. And when you referred to him as her insurance friend she let it stand."

"Because it was a point she wasn't talking on at all. I wonder if she'd still be alive if she had."

Tad's shrug was his only answer. They rode in silence until they were clear of Medfield. Then Madden said, "Miss Sheldon's an attractive girl. Seems very nice, too."

"Yes." Tad's tone was neutral.

"Doesn't mean, though, that she couldn't have smothered Mrs. Meeker last night."

"No." Tad was still neutral.

The inspector let it go. He said, "It will take a little time to get them all sorted out. At the moment it's Johnston who stands out, complete with motive."

"Do you think he ever looked for Arthur Williams at all?"

"At a guess, I'd say you could put in your eye the amount of time he's spent looking for Williams; and the amount of honest information we'll get on him from Johnston's reports."

"In other words, we'll have about what we have now: grandson of an old friend thought to be in Texas or maybe Timbuktu. Young, presumably, being a grandson."

"Young's a relative term," Madden reminded him. "Applied to the grandson of one of Mrs. Meeker's contemporaries, it could mean any age up to the middle thirties or so." He paused. "I don't think Williams is that old, though. Somehow—I don't know how—what she said gave me the impression he wasn't more than in his early twenties."

"I got that impression too," Tad said. After a moment's thought he added, "But not of a Williams father or mother."

"Good point. Particularly the father. He'd be the son of her old friend, a closer link than the grandson. He must be dead."

"Which would make Arthur Williams at least a half orphan," Tad said on the same thoughtful note.

"The scholarship fund?"

"Uh-huh. I know Thayer said the applications all came to him, but what if Williams, because of her old friendship with his grandfather, applied directly to Mrs. Meeker?"

"I'll take it up with Thayer."

Tad looked modestly pleased with himself. Then, not to

bask in success, he said, "This is April Fools' Day. Things don't have to be what they seem."

Madden smiled. "Even what looks like murder? In this case, I think we'll find it was."

He fell silent after he said this, his thoughts on death, a date—predestined?—when it must come to one and all. To Mrs. Meeker, April 1, 1960.

For him, what date unheeded year after year?

For Estelle, his wife, the date had been September 9. They had been married in September too. September 18.

No use, though, to think of Estelle's death or man's common destiny. It depressed him.

Chapter Seven

OVER the weekend Mrs. Meeker's death made head-
lines in every newspaper the postal inspector saw. Monday
morning's paper said that the coroner hadn't yet received a
report from the pathologist performing the autopsy; that
Chief Pauling would make no comment on what the report
might contain, but by judging from the amount of time the
Medfield Police Department was devoting to the case, Mrs.
Meeker had not died from natural causes; that private funeral
services for her would be held Tuesday afternoon at Hilltop
House, her late residence in Medfield.

Soon after he reached his office Monday morning, Madden
put in a call to Chief Pauling and arranged to see him at
police headquarters later in the morning.

Pauling had nothing to report on Johnston. "We've can-
vassed every insurance agent in Medfield," he added. "None
of them recommended him to Mrs. Meeker. Never heard of
him, they all say."

"Well, I suppose I'd better see what the Hartford insurance
companies offer on him."

"He never existed as an insurance investigator except for
Mrs. Meeker's benefit," Pauling stated.

"No, he didn't. But I'd better make that official, just the
same."

Tad was given the Hartford assignment. He was to go to
insurance-company claim departments, Madden told him.
Perhaps one would be enough; they must have some sort of

centralized system for the exchange of information on insurance investigators.

Right after Tad left the inspector drove to Medfield.

He found Pauling in his office. The police chief had the Johnston file ready for him. "I haven't had much time to give to it," he said, "but just from reading it, it looks like a real fraud case to me." He handed the file to Madden and shook his head. "I can't imagine Mrs. Meeker being taken in by it."

"She wanted to be." The inspector glanced through the file. It contained Johnston's reports and expense accounts, statements from the Dunston bank in which Mrs. Meeker had opened a checking account June 30, 1959, and canceled checks made out to Johnston and paid through the Bronx branch of a New York bank. There were no copies of Mrs. Meeker's letters to Johnston. They had been handwritten. She had kept Joan Sheldon in the dark about them.

"I sent a man to the Dunston bank this morning," Pauling said. "All told, she put eighty-five thousand into the account. She made one deposit of fifty thousand last September and withdrew it in November. You'll notice the last statement shows there's something under five thousand left in the account."

Madden looked at the statements for each month. Then he said, "Well, wherever she has her safe-deposit box the signature card will tell us if she put the fifty thousand back with that other million or two."

"My God, when you think of it." Pauling shook his head.

"I'd rather not," Madden said. "Makes me feel underprivileged. How is your investigation going?"

The police chief had mostly negative results to report. Along with Medfield insurance agents, friends and acquaintances of Mrs. Meeker's denied knowledge of Johnston and said that they had not recommended him to her. Inquiries regarding strangers, loiterers, parked cars, anyone or anything out of the ordinary in Mrs. Meeker's neighborhood the night of her death had been fruitless.

"But hell," said Pauling, "a regiment could camp on her grounds and not be seen from the road." He paused, brows drawn into a frown. "I don't say it means anything but Peck's got a record. Drew a two-year sentence in Massachusetts in 1920 for assault with a deadly weapon. Put a guy in the hospital for three months. It grew out of a drunken brawl when he was just a kid, he says, and he's never been in trouble since. But it's a record; it can't be changed."

"What about the others?"

"They all get ten, fifteen thousand in the old lady's will. Aside from that, I've nothing to go on with them. Mrs. Peck's lived in Medfield all her life. Thayer, I'm told, does a fine job with the scholarship fund and is well respected in the educational world. He seems to be out of it, anyway. We checked the Putnam through the Philadelphia P.D. and Thayer stayed there last Thursday night, leaving his car in the hotel garage from five-thirty P.M. Thursday until quarter of seven Friday morning. On Miss Sheldon I get good reports all around. Excellent student in high school and at Bay Path, very well liked, regarded as a real nice girl. Hardly the type to kill the old lady to get her out of the way and make sure of her legacy at the same time.

"There are two great-nieces out in Oregon who get more than the rest. But they didn't kill Mrs. Meeker from that distance. A few friends around here inherit a little something but we've got nothing to show they killed her."

"Enemies?"

Pauling shrugged. "You met her. She walked all over people but it doesn't mean they sneaked in her house and killed her."

"Through a door conveniently unlocked," Madden supplemented.

"That damn door," said the police chief.

"A gift horse to be viewed with suspicion." Madden's dark face wore a meditative look. "If there was collusion between an outside murderer and a member of the household it would be an elementary precaution to check on the door later. And it makes a very poor red herring for an inside job. Much better to break a cellar window."

"Don't forget, there was the hope it would pass for a natural death," Pauling reminded him.

"Well, with a house as big as that there must be at least one cellar window that wouldn't be noticed right away unless there was a police investigation."

"Yeah. And a pane of glass isn't hard to——"

The telephone interrupted him. He scooped up the receiver and said, "Police chief," into the mouthpiece, and then, "Oh yes, Mr. Benson. I was hoping I'd hear from you today."

With his free hand he pulled a pad and pencil toward him and began to make notes as he listened, saying, "Uh-huh" and "I see" at intervals.

At last he said, "Well, thank you for calling, Mr. Benson. Although there was no doubt in my mind and we've been handling it as one I'm glad to have it made official."

He hung up. "Coroner," he said to Madden. "He's just heard from the pathologist who says Mrs. Meeker apparently died from suffocation." Pauling looked at his notes. "Many minute hemorrhages in the lungs; particles of lint and thread in the mouth and nostrils. Scrapings from the bed linen identical with the lint and thread found in the nasal and oral cavities. No other cause of death apparent. Trachea clear of mucus and foreign objects. Brain examined for thrombosis, clot or hemorrhage. No signs of these, no gross hemorrhage of lungs, heart, brain or stomach." He paused. "That's about it. Oh, the time of death. The duration of the digestive process varies, the pathologist says, but the empty stomach and the findings in the upper gastrointestinal tract indicate that Mrs. Meeker died several hours after her seven-o'clock dinner. Probably around midnight, give or take an hour either way."

Pauling paused again. "So there it is," he said. "Not your problem, of course, unless Johnston and the murderer are one and the same."

They discussed this possibility. However likely it was, Pauling said, he couldn't limit himself to it. He had to look for other prospects, other motives until more conclusive evidence pointing to Johnston came to light. Madden, with his investigation centered on the fraud, said that tomorrow he would go to the Bronx bank through which Mrs. Meeker's checks to Johnston had cleared.

Arthur Williams had to be located, they agreed. He might have been in collusion with Johnston on the fraud; he might be Mrs. Meeker's murderer or have played some part in her death. This was Madden's suggestion; the police chief shook his head over it. If Arthur Williams was involved in the fraud or the murder, then he too had another identity. No one the Medfield police had questioned professed to know any more about him than about Johnston.

Scholarship applicant? Pauling looked doubtful. Madden explained that he was thinking of an application sent directly to Mrs. Meeker. Then he asked to use the phone and called Brian Thayer, who said that he was just leaving to keep a lunch date but would be home by two o'clock.

Madden said that he would see him at two and made another call, this one to Mrs. Meeker's lawyers. Mr. Hohlbein was out for the day, but Mr. Garth would be free at one-thirty. The secretary's tone indicated that an appointment at such short notice was a concession for which Madden should be duly grateful.

He inferred that Hohlbein and Garth were high-priced lawyers.

He had lunch with Pauling. Promptly at one-thirty he entered Hohlbein and Garth's elegant suite of offices in Medfield's newest professional building.

He disliked Garth on sight, conservative clothes and haircut, smile a shade too earnestly boyish for a man who must be well into his thirties, handclasp too consciously quick and firm. Youngish man on the make, Madden labeled him, and was ready to guess that in a correct, not too pushing fashion, the junior partner of the firm had political ambitions; that Mrs. Garth would be impeccably suitable as the wife of a rising young lawyer; that there were three children, two boys and a girl; that she was active in the Woman's Club and he in Lions, Rotary, and Jaycee; and finally, that neither of them had harbored an unorthodox opinion since their wedding day.

Madden knew that he could be completely wrong about all this, but also knew that he would go right on disliking Garth.

Garth was prepared to be helpful in what he referred to with fastidious distaste as this unfortunate Johnston affair, which would not, he said more than once, have ever come about if Mrs. Meeker had only seen fit to consult Mr. Hohlbein or him about it.

Madden regretted not being able to find fault with so true a statement. He asked to see a copy of Mrs. Meeker's will.

Garth brought one out.

The date, October 8, 1957, immediately caught the inspector's eye. "Fairly recent," he remarked. "Was she in the habit of making new wills?"

"Oh no. She had reason to change the one she made right

after Mr. Meeker's death. Her estate had grown considerably. She wanted to make a more equitable distribution of it among the groups that would benefit the most; particularly the scholarship fund. At the time the will was drawn Mr. Hohlbein mentioned to me how mentally alert she seemed for her age, knowing just what changes she wanted made and so forth."

Garth hesitated. "Mr. Hohlbein and I have noticed some lapses since, though. Most of them this past year, I'd say. Even two or three years ago I doubt that she'd have become involved in this unfortunate Johnston affair. She'd have consulted us, you see. She always did before, and showed the utmost confidence in whatever we advised."

The inspector nodded, doubting this. Mrs. Meeker hadn't struck him as ready to seek anyone's advise, least of all Garth's. With her sharp tongue she'd have cut his pompousness to ribbons. It would have been Hohlbein who handled her affairs.

Madden settled back to read the will.

He skimmed over the millions that went to Meeker Park, Medfield Hospital, the civic center, the Public Health Nursing Association, the library, and so on, pausing when he came to the scholarship fund. Two millions were added to what had been set aside for it in Mrs. Meeker's lifetime, and the proviso made that as long as Brian Thayer continued to discharge his duties as administrator of the fund to the satisfaction of the board of trustees (hereinafter appointed by the bank administering the estate) he was to be retained in his present capacity at a salary commensurate with the increased responsibilities enlargement of the fund would entail.

A splendid vote of confidence in Thayer, Madden reflected. Tenure, too. Very nice for him.

He went on to personal bequests, a list of names largely unknown to him. Twenty-five thousand to each of the great-nieces in Oregon (not much to blood relatives out of millions) ten thousand to this friend and that, five thousand to another; to Brian Thayer, the sum of ten thousand dollars; to the Pecks, ten thousand each; to Joan Sheldon the conditional bequest of ten thousand to be paid to her in the event that she was still in Mrs. Meeker's employ at the time of the latter's death. (No additional five thousand for each year after Joan's twenty-first birthday; Mrs. Meeker hadn't got around to taking care of that.)

Too bad, Madden thought. Joan Sheldon had earned the larger bequest.

Mr. Hohlbein was left twenty thousand, Garth ten. There were no other names Madden recognized. Arthur Williams's might well have been included, he felt. Mrs. Meeker had spent a small fortune on a search for him but had made no provision for him in her will if he should be found after her death, and had never mentioned his name to her lawyers.

Madden took up this point with Garth, who shrugged it off. "Old people have their idiosyncrasies."

"This one came a bit high at thirty thousand or more."

"Well, she had a number of them where money was concerned," Garth said. "Sometimes we'd have trouble persuading her to make tax-exempt charitable contributions, and I've known her to quarrel with a plumber over a bill for fixing a faucet; the next moment she'd put another half million into the scholarship fund or thirty thousand into something as impractical as this unfortunate Johnston affair. There was no telling how she'd react to spending money."

Madden inquired next about the audit of the scholarship fund.

There was an annual audit, Garth informed him. No discrepancies or shortages had ever been found. Brian Thayer was a thoroughly honest and competent administrator. His salary had reached the ten thousand mark. His expenses ran another four or five thousand. The lawyer didn't know him very well although he saw him occasionally at some dinner party—Thayer, like himself, Madden reflected, was the extra man so prized by hostesses—and found him easy enough to talk to. But he didn't play golf, didn't seem to belong to any local clubs—his work took him away a lot, of course—which probably accounted for his tendency to keep to himself.

Garth's glance began to flicker to his watch.

He said that he had already told the police chief that he didn't know what insurance man had recommended Johnston to Mrs. Meeker. He would offer no theory to account for her murder. The whole thing, his manner conveyed, was so far outside the normal routine of Hohlbein and Garth that it practically demanded being swept under the rug.

No doubt Mrs. Meeker had snubbed him many a time and he felt no grief over her passing. Even so, Madden's dislike of the suave, correct lawyer deepened. It would be all right with him, he decided, if his investigation of the fraud, with its probable by-product of murder, led to Garth's door. Motive? Ten-thousand-dollar bequest. At first glance, not much of a motive for a man of his standing; but for all his air of affluence, who could tell what his private financial picture was?

The inspector knew as he left that this was wishful thinking. Nevertheless, he made a mental note to look into Garth's financial background.

Brian Thayer had a downtown address. He lived in an apartment house not over three or four years old, a reclaimed island of landscaped brick and glass on the fringe of the business district.

He occupied a two-bedroom apartment on the fourth floor,

using the second bedroom as his office. Airy and bright, the apartment was furnished with good modern furniture, rugs, and draperies. Done by a professional decorator, Madden thought, and somehow as impersonal, as unremarkable as its occupant. In Dunston the rent would run close to two hundred a month; in Medfield, perhaps twenty-five less, not all of it paid by Thayer, who could charge off one room on his expense account.

He took Madden into the room he used as an office. It contained a desk, files, a typewriter on a stand, and two big leather armchairs. A newspaper open at stock-market reports lay on one of them. Thayer folded it up and offered a drink.

The inspector declined. To begin the interview, he asked if Thayer, with more time to think it over, could add to what he had said the other day about Johnston.

Thayer shook his head. "It's all I think about, too. That and her death. It's still unbelievable that it was murder. For all her domineering ways, I can't conceive of her having had a deadly enemy."

He went on to explain in his precise voice that he'd always got along with her pretty well himself. Theirs was primarily a business relationship, but over the years it had included some personal contact, occasional dinners at Hilltop House, some confidences exchanged, some discussions of problems unconnected with the scholarship fund. Mrs. Meeker had given him much latitude with the fund, he added. It was his province.

Madden, as he listened, found Brian Thayer too detached, too cold and aloof, and decided that he didn't like him any better than Garth.

Was it his own fault? he asked himself presently. Was he having an off day when no one could please him?

They went on to the administration of the scholarship fund.

"Let me show you a form." Thayer went to one of the files and brought out a printed application form and a folder. He handed the folder to Madden first. "This explains the requirements for eligibility."

The folder listed the usual qualifications of scholastic standing and need and the additional qualification that the applicant must be male and a full orphan through the death or desertion of both parents. A further clause stated that the stipends of the scholarships would be adjusted to individual need and would be paid directly to the recipient, who was to make his own arrangements for admission to the institution for higher study of his choice.

The application form was standard in the information it requested except that it asked for the date and place of the death or desertion of the applicant's parents.

Madden laid the material aside. "Aren't most scholarships paid to the college rather than the student?"

"Yes, as a rule. But Mrs. Meeker felt that it cultivated a sense of independence, self-reliance, for the recipients to handle their own money."

The precise way he had of speaking was one of the offputting things about him, Madden decided.

Thayer went on to say that there were, of course, safeguards in the form of periodic checks with the college to make sure the scholarship stipend was being used for its intended purpose; there had been no case of a recipient misusing his stipend. It was very rare for one of them to fail at college. Indeed, most of the recipients were near the top of their class; making the dean's list was a commonplace among them.

His voice took on a platform note as he continued in this

vein. Madden could visualize him giving complacent talks on the Ulysses S. Meeker Memorial Scholarship Fund to P.T.A.s, club and faculty groups, and student bodies, letting it be understood that much of the credit for the fund's successes redounded to its administrator.

Madden got in a question. "But the trustees make the final decision on what applicants will be accepted, don't they?"

Slightly less complacent, Thayer said they did. "Only the final decision, though," he added. "Last year, for example, there were ten scholarships available and twenty-six eligible applicants. I weeded them out and presented a list of sixteen that I considered the cream of the crop to the trustees. This year—the meeting was three weeks ago—there were eighteen. I go over the list with the trustees and the decisions are made." He shook his head. "A great responsibility, really, when you think that a young man's whole future may hinge on a recommendation of yours."

"Yes, I imagine it is," Madden agreed. Then he asked, "Hasn't anyone ever found out that Mrs. Meeker had the final say on the scholarships and applied directly to her?"

"No," Thayer said stiffly. "It would be most irregular. It's never happened."

The inspector's glance strayed to the filing cabinets. "How long do you keep rejected applications?"

"So far I've kept them all for the eight years the fund has been in existence. We should set up a policy on destroying them after a certain period of time. In fact, I brought it up at a trustees' meeting last fall but no decision was made. The trustees meet only two or three times a year. Mrs. Meeker, as chairman, called the meetings."

"What I have in mind," Madden said, "is the possibility that Arthur Williams was, after all, a scholarship applicant. That he knew of Mrs. Meeker's friendship with his grandfather and applied directly to her. Would she necessarily have mentioned it to you if she turned him down for some reason she wanted to keep to herself? Then let's say she regretted it but found that he'd moved away and left no forwarding address when she wrote to him again at the address he'd given her."

"Out of the question," Brian Thayer retorted. "She would not have gone over my head that way. She left administration matters entirely in my hands. Arthur Williams, whoever he is, had no connection with a scholarship. Her interest in him was a personal one."

Touchy ego, Madden thought. He said mildly, "Well then, let's consider another possibility, Mr. Thayer. You must have hundreds of applications in your files. Couldn't you have forgotten Arthur Williams ever applied if you rejected his application yourself at some preliminary stage?"

"I'll show you the rejects." Thayer went to a file and opened a drawer labeled "R–Z" on the guide insert. He took out a bundle of folders and brought them to Madden. "If you'd care to look, Inspector, these are rejected Ws in alphabetical order."

Madden gave him a cool, deliberate stare and looked. Woburn followed Wiley. No Williamses at all. Without comment he handed the folders back to Thayer and got leisurely to his feet. "Thank you, Mr. Thayer," he said.

"Not at all." Thayer had recovered his detachment. "I'm sorry your theory about Williams turned out to be wrong."

He wasn't sorry, though, Madden reflected as he went out to the self-service elevator. Mustn't wound his ego; that was where he lived; that was where any warmth he had was located.

Honesty compelled Madden to admit that perhaps his own mood was too carping; perhaps it colored his judgment of Thayer.

Chapter Eight

BACK in Dunston in the late afternoon the inspector sat down at his desk with the Johnston file. He began his study of it with the canceled checks, comparing Johnston's signature on the letters to Mrs. Meeker with his signature on the checks. Under a magnifying glass they appeared identical to Madden; the Bureau in Washington would give him an expert opinion on this.

None of the checks had "For deposit only" written above Johnston's signature. He wouldn't have neglected this precaution if he'd mailed them to his bank, Madden thought, turning his attention to the endorsements. There were four on each of them; Johnston's bank, the Federal Reserve Bank of New York, the Federal Reserve Bank of Boston, and the Dunston bank on which they were drawn. Apparently Johnston had taken all of Mrs. Meeker's checks to his bank in person. None had been mailed in, none had been cashed in the Midwest or Southwest where he was supposed to have been when the checks were mailed to and cashed by him.

Madden turned to the reports. Their envelopes hadn't been kept but they were in chronological order, the first one, from Somerville, Iowa, dated July 17, 1959. It took up three type-written pages. Mrs. Meeker had said that, coming from her home town, it was an honest report, the only honest one Johnston had sent her.

It began with a reference to a previous letter written on Johnston's arrival in Somerville.

The letter wasn't in the file. If all it had said was, Arrived to-day and will begin investigation tomorrow, Mrs. Meeker had probably not bothered to keep it, even though she had told Madden that she had kept everything Johnston had written to her.

Madden had to let it go. He went on with the report.

Much of the information in it must have been already known to Mrs. Meeker. In substance, it said that Arthur Williams, grandfather of subject, had left Somerville around 1900 with his parents and moved to San Antonio, Texas. A few years later he had married a San Antonio girl whose name had been forgotten by Johnston's Somerville informant. His parents had died in San Antonio. His only child was a son James born before World War I. In 1919 or 1920 the son had visited a cousin, now dead, in Somerville. No descendants of the cousin's family could be located. No further information was obtainable in Somerville except that subject's grandfather was believed to have died in Texas close to forty years ago. An elderly lady, name given, stated that, as she recalled it, at the time of his death Arthur Williams no longer lived in San Antonio but elsewhere in Texas. However, the report concluded, San Antonio seemed the likeliest place to continue his inquiries and Johnston was going there from Somerville.

His name was signed with a small *b* below it, indicating that he hadn't signed it himself. Another public stenographer, Madden thought.

Johnston's expense account meticulously listed expenses on the drive to Iowa from Hartford and for his stay in Somerville. Except that he seemed to have lingered there too long considering the meagerness of the information he gathered, the first expense account Johnston submitted didn't seem particularly excessive.

He played his fish gently at the start, Madden reflected, reaching for a sheet of paper and setting down the dates of arrival and departure from Somerville.

Mrs. Meeker had already turned over to the postal inspector Johnston's second report, sent the first week of August 1959 from San Antonio. Referring to it, Madden set down the date of Johnston's arrival there.

The third report, dated from San Antonio a fortnight later, found Johnston preparing to leave for Dallas, school records indicating James Williams's transfer to a school in that city in October 1919.

Johnston stated that since his last report he had been engaged in house-to-house inquiries on two streets where subject's grandfather, according to tax records and city directories, had lived between 1909 and 1919. He had located two women, names given, who remembered subject's father and grandfather but did not know what had become of them after they left San Antonio.

Again an initial beneath Johnston's signature indicated that he had not signed the report.

The attached expense account listed expenses over a hundred dollars higher than the previous report.

This pattern continued, Madden discovered, making notes on his sheet of paper. In Dallas, Houston, Amarillo, Johnston listed expenses that grew and grew.

His reports were mostly pure fiction, the inspector thought, trimmed with such occasional facts as a copy of Arthur Williams's death certificate from Dallas, where he had died of nephritis on April 18, 1921. A copy of a birth certificate for Arthur Henry Williams, born in Houston December 11, 1940, son of James and Gertrude Williams, enclosed with one report was disavowed as the wrong Arthur Williams in the next.

It gave Madden an idea of his age. Not more than nineteen or twenty.

According to the reports, he was a restless young man, always on the move, working one month at a garage in Amarillo—positively identified from his picture by the proprietor —and the next month as a bus boy in New Mexico. It was November when Johnston reported tracing him that far. December found him headed for Gary, Indiana, where he had a friend working in a steel mill.

Meanwhile, the fish was being played on an ever-tightening line. A graph of Johnston's expense account, using July 1959 as a base, would have shown a steady rise to almost double the original amount by January 1960.

Reports from Gary emphasized a round of inquiries at employment agencies, plant personnel offices, garages, and restaurants. Hotel bills, meals, tips, stenographic services, car expenses—four new tires in December, an expensive repair job in January—all were included, subject to Johnston's particular brand of inflation.

Mid-February found him in Detroit. According to his report, Arthur Williams, elusive and restless as ever, had worked only three weeks in Gary and then moved on to Detroit to try his luck in the auto industry. (Mrs. Meeker should have lost interest in such a rolling stone as this, Madden reflected. Ulysses S. Meeker had got started on the road to millions by staying put.)

This report, like all the others, had an initial under Johnston's signature to show that whoever had typed it had signed it for him. It couldn't be chance that he had signed none of the reports himself; it must be wariness of putting his signature on record.

The March report from Detroit that had been Johnston's undoing was the last of them. When Madden had read it he put the file in order and added it to the folder he had started on the case. The notes he had made went into his pocket.

It was almost six-thirty, with the office long deserted. Tad had returned from Hartford two hours ago bringing back the report that no Hartford insurance company had ever employed Johnston as an investigator or had him listed as one.

That evening, after dinner at a restaurant, the inspector settled himself in an easy chair in his apartment with a can of beer beside him and studied the notes he had made from the Johnston file. He would have summaries made from them in the morning, he decided, and through division headquarters in Boston air-mail requests, to inspectors in the cities the reports had come from to find out whatever they could about Johnston. Hotel signature cards could be picked up, names mentioned in the reports checked, and so forth. Some information, some sort of pattern on Johnston should come from it.

Madden had a second can of beer and went to bed. His last thought on the case was that Johnston, faking his reports, had done much coming and going in the expanses of the Southwest. Far more than seemed practical by car. He'd better ask that airline manifests be checked.

Chapter Nine

MADDEN cleared his request for assistance from other postal inspectors through division headquarters and dictated the summaries to be air-mailed to them as soon as he reached his desk the next morning. He was ready to leave for the Bronx bank when Pauling phoned him.

The police chief said that he now had a complete picture of Mrs. Meeker's accounts, checking and saving, in Medfield banks. The fifty thousand withdrawn from Dunston had not been deposited in Medfield or put in her safe-deposit box. Her signature card showed no visit to it since September 10, 1959, when she had probably taken the money out; at least she had deposited fifty thousand in her Dunston checking account that day.

"In cash?" Madden asked.

"Yes. Withdrew it in cash, too, November 17."

"Well . . ." said Madden. Then, thinking aloud, "I wonder if she gave it to Johnston. If she did, she was lying when she told me she'd never met him. She wouldn't have mailed it to him in cash; he'd have had to be on hand for her to turn it over to him." He hesitated. "And yet I didn't get the impression she was lying the one time I saw her. Withholding some things, yes, but not lying. I'm going to his bank today. His account may tell us if he got the money from her."

Pauling's sigh came clearly over the wire. "Something better tell us something," he said. "I feel as if I'm getting nowhere. FBI has no later record on Peck; nothing new on his wife or Thayer or the Sheldon girl. Nothing on any of the others I've checked so far who get legacies from the estate."

"How about Hohlbein and Garth? They're legatees. Have you checked their financial standing?"

"Why——" The police chief sounded startled. "Well, not yet."

"No one's immune," Madden pointed out, and grinned at the thought of how outraged Garth would be if he could hear this suggestion.

Pauling inquired, "You get anything new from Garth or Thayer yesterday?"

"Nothing worth my time. Chandler's trip to Hartford, though, confirmed what we already knew about Johnston. He's a complete fake as an insurance investigator." Madden went on, "What about Miss Sheldon's boy friends? Any chance one of them could be Johnston?"

Out of the tail of his eye he saw that Tad, propped against the desk waiting for him to finish, looked very blank indeed; less so when Madden added, "Or someone in the Pecks' circle or Thayer's?"

"I'm checking on all that," Pauling said. "Takes time. This afternoon I'll have to pull men off other assignments to cover Mrs. Meeker's funeral. There'll be a crowd at the cemetery and outside the house no matter how private the services are supposed to be. Well, we'll see what develops."

Pauling's voice was heavy with the responsibility Mrs. Meeker's murder laid on him. He said good-by and hung up.

Madden and Tad Chandler set out for the Bronx. Before they were long on the way, Tad asked, "Have you got a favorite at Mrs. Meeker's for a tie-in with Johnston?"

"No, not yet. Lots to find out first. Of course, Peck's prison record means that Pauling is taking a very close look at him."

"Nobody ever really lives it down if his foot slips," Tad remarked.

"No. We carry the past, good or bad, on our backs all our days." A moment later, in a lighter tone, Madden added, "But you don't even know you have a past yet."

"It's as light as a feather," Tad assured him cheerfully.

Madden glanced at the young, clear-cut face on which time had yet to write and said, "Just the same, I doubt that Miss Sheldon is mixed up in this."

Tad brightened. "So do I."

After Madden identified himself at the Bronx bank, he was turned over to one of the officers and Johnston's ledger card was produced. Madden brought out Mrs. Meeker's canceled checks. Beginning with August 11, 1959, when Johnston had opened a savings account, each deposit was checked against Mrs. Meeker's payments to him. The fifty thousand withdrawn from her Dunston account was not among them. Total deposits from August to March totaled $26,585.00. Withdrawals over the same period followed no regular pattern and left a current balance of something over nine hundred dollars. Except for bank drafts payable to Miss Lazinski, all withdrawals had been made in cash.

Johnston had given the bank his Hartford mailing address.

The inspector, copying dates and amounts of deposits and withdrawals from the ledger card, pointed out to Tad that Johnston had been in and out of the bank often enough to indicate that his real address was within reasonable driving distance of it. He had probably opened a savings instead of a checking account because he would have had so few checks to write under the name of Johnston that the bank's attention might have been drawn to the inactivity of his account.

Tellers who had waited on him were questioned by Madden. None could give the postal inspector a description of him. He had been an unobtrusive customer. Records showed no safe-deposit box under his name.

Madden arranged to have local police summoned to hold him for questioning in the doubtful event that he ever appeared at the bank again. Then, supplied with a photostatic copy of Johnston's signature card, Madden was ready to leave.

He would sent it to the Questioned Documents Examiner in Washington, he told Tad on the way to his car. With it would go one of Johnston's letters to Mrs. Meeker and checks he had endorsed.

"Do you want the signatures compared because you think there may be more than one person mixed up in this?" Tad inquired.

"I don't know," Madden replied. "Let's just put it that I want to make sure they're from a common source."

They'd had lunch before they went to the bank. It was close to four o'clock when they left, and Madden suggested stopping for coffee before they returned to Dunston. Seated opposite Tad in a luncheonette booth, he took out the copy of Johnston's signature card and handed it across the table. "Take a good look at the writing," he said. "Notice the hesitancies in forming the loops on the j and the y, the general effect of having been copied or at least written with more than average care. The same characteristics show up in the signature on the letter and the endorsements on the checks. The Bureau will tell me if they had a common source and if the handwriting was disguised or written with the off-hand."

Coffee and the pie Tad had ordered were set before them. When the waitress left, Madden continued, "If the report I get back confirms common source and disguised or off-hand writing, then I proceed on the assumption that Johnston is someone close enough to Mrs. Meeker to have his handwriting examined if the question of fraud came up." He paused for a cautious sip of his steaming hot coffee and then said, "Someone who looked ahead and made very careful plans to guard against detection."

"But couldn't avoid signing his name sometimes," Tad said. "Awful pie."

"Naturally. A quick-lunch place." The inspector smiled as he saw that Tad was making inroads on the pie in spite of what he said about it. He was still young enough to eat almost anything set in front of him.

"If it's disguised or off-hand writing, you going to get specimens from all those people in Medfield?" Tad inquired.

"Oh yes, regardless of what the writing is. But I'll wait for the Bureau's report. I'll ask them to expedite it. I don't think of this as just another fraud case. I think it was fraud and murder with the murder committed to cover up the fraud."

Madden, after he said this, fell silent while he drank his coffee. Tad drank his and finished eating the pie.

Driving back to Dunston through countryside showing the first green of spring, Madden brought up the case again, saying that he thought the fifty thousand Mrs. Meeker had taken out of her Dunston account fitted into the fraud somewhere.

"Making almost eighty thousand Johnston took her for," Tad remarked.

"Yes. It was in cash, remember, so it didn't have to go through his account. He's got a safe-deposit box somewhere —God only knows in what bank or under what name. He had to open the Bronx account to cash Mrs. Meeker's checks but he's been taking the money out almost as fast as he put it in. Now that's probably in his safe-deposit box too."

"Unless he's got it spread around in several different banks under his real name. Have to be several. Isn't ten thousand the maximum they insure?"

"I can't see him doing that. I think it's in a box. He's so careful he'd realize that bank records, everything down in black and white, have led to many a criminal's downfall." In a solemnly paternal tone Madden continued, "Always put money you steal in a safe-deposit box, Tad, under a different name. Much harder to catch up with you that way."

"I'll remember," Tad said with a grin.

Chapter Ten

THE postal inspector went alone to Hartford the next day, leaving Tad to inquire at Dunston banks for an account or safe-deposit box in Mrs. Meeker's name, Johnston's, or any of the others connected with her, not excluding her attorneys. This wasn't an assignment very likely to produce positive results, Madden explained to Tad; but if it did nothing else, it forwarded the process of elimination.

On this visit to Miss Lazinski, Madden immediately introduced himself and brought out his identification folder.

She looked at the folder and asked him to sit down, adding, "Are you still trying to locate Mr. Johnston?"

"Yes." Madden seated himself and put away the folder.

A worried expression came to her face. "I haven't seen or heard from him since you were here before."

"I'm not surprised. I didn't think you would." Madden's smile offered reassurance. "I came to see what you could tell me about him."

Miss Lazinski was seated at her desk. She picked up a notebook, laid it down. "Is he in serious trouble?" she asked.

"I don't know how serious it is yet. I haven't been able to get hold of him to find out what his side of the story is." He paused. "What makes you assume right away that it's serious, Miss Lazinski, instead of some routine thing?"

"Well . . ." The worried look on her plain, rather heavy face deepened. "After you were here before I got to thinking you were the first person that ever came to ask for him all this time. Then there's his phone"—her gesture indicated the telephone on a corner table that Madden had noticed on his earlier visit—"which he pays for every month and doesn't need in the least. Very little mail, too." Her voice fell away on an uncertain note. After a moment she said, "I've never had a client like him before."

The inspector produced cigarettes. "How'd you get him for a client?" he asked. "Let's take it right from the beginning."

She hesitated. "I don't know what I should say. Not that I could tell you much, but after all, he is paying me and——"

"Miss Lazinski, he's mixed up in a fraud case. Getting money out of an old lady in Medfield. She died last week under peculiar circumstances." Madden avoided the word murder. The coroner's findings hadn't been released yet. He said, "I need all the information I can get on Johnston."

Miss Lazinski stared at him. "That wealthy old lady the newspapers say was murdered?"

"Yes, that one. Mrs. Meeker."

Miss Lazinski turned pale. "About all the mail Mr. Johnston ever had came from Medfield. Very good stationery with an engraved return address. A house——"

"Hilltop House."

"Yes, that was it. There's been none lately, though, and her name wasn't on the envelopes. So when I read about her I never dreamed——"

"No reason you should," Madden said. "Even so, I wonder if, perhaps without realizing it, you haven't been a little uneasy about Johnston for quite a while."

She was silent, turning her cigarette between her fingers. Presently she sighed. "I guess you're right. Bank drafts instead of a check——"

"The beginning," Madden reminded her.

"Yes . . ." She sighed again. "A year ago last January I ran an ad when a couple of people dropped off my mailing service list. Mr. Johnston came to see me. He was interested in the mailing service, he said, but he also wanted his own phone installed and phone answering service too. I told him I'd never made an arrangement like that and wouldn't consider it because his calls would take me from my work and there'd be no one to take them at night. He said he'd have no calls at night and might not have one a month during the day; they would be important calls, though, when they came, and he wanted them taken on his own phone."

Miss Lazinski, searching her memory, spoke slowly. She went on, "He didn't plan to pick up his mail himself, he said, he wanted it forwarded. There wouldn't be much of it, either, for the next several months. He was an insurance investigator and he'd taken on a case that would keep him out of town indefinitely. He offered me fifty a month. So I said yes."

She turned to look at the phone on the corner table. "He had it installed the next week, about the last week of January. He said he was leaving town the next day and had me order the phone right then and there and find out how much the installation charge would be. He paid me two months in advance for mailing and phone service and the installation charge and two months in advance on the phone bill." After a pause she added, "In cash."

"Didn't you find that a bit unusual?"

"He said someone had just paid him in cash."

"Oh. And then he gave you a forwarding address?"

"I have it right here." Miss Lazinski took a card out of her desk and read off a West Fifty-second Street number in New York. Then she said, "He's never had much mail. The first few months, not more than three or four letters altogether. They all had a Hartford postmark."

"Do you recall if there was a return address?"

"None of them had one. Just plain envelopes. Typed." She smiled apologetically. "I don't make it a practice to study my clients' mail but I noticed his because there was so little of it. And no phone calls at all. I thought he wasn't getting his money's worth. Then, when the two months were up I got a bank draft from a New York bank paying for my services and the phone bill for another two months in advance. It was beginning to bother me. I wrote a note telling him he'd had no phone calls and asking if he wanted to keep the phone after the next two months. Weeks later he wrote back saying he wanted to keep the phone and not to worry about it. The letter had a New York postmark."

"Was it typed?"

"Yes."

"Have you still got it?"

Miss Lazinski shook her head. "It didn't seem important. It went into the wastebasket."

She went on with her story. Starting last summer, Mr. Johnston began to receive letters postmarked Medfield and kept receiving them regularly about every two weeks thereafter. The letters in plain envelopes with a Hartford postmark continued to come at intervals.

Letters Johnston mailed to himself for Miss Lazinski's benefit, Madden thought.

"That's all the mail he's ever received," she said next. "He told me to throw out advertising matter so I don't count that. He hasn't even been getting his Medfield letters the last three or four weeks. There won't be any more of them now, will there?"

"No. They came from Mrs. Meeker."

"Perhaps she was the one who called him three or four weeks ago. The only phone call he's had—except solicitors—the whole time he's been paying for the phone. It was a person-to-person call from Medfield, a woman who wanted to know where she could reach Mr. Johnston by phone."

That was Mrs. Meeker, Madden thought.

"I told her I didn't know just where to reach him at the moment. I wanted to sound efficient and helpful—it was about time I earned the money he paid me—so I said he'd been in Hartford March 10 but now he was away again and that if she cared to leave a message I'd see that it reached him. But she wasn't interested. She wanted to locate him right away and there was nothing I could do about that. I was just to forward his mail, you see. He'd told me to give no one his New York address."

"You saw him March 10?"

"No, I didn't. But I knew he'd been in Hartford that day because he stopped by here to see me. I found a note from him pushed through the mail slot the next morning. It was just a penciled note written on an envelope that he'd put the money for his next payment in. It said he must have just missed me and as he'd be leaving early in the morning he might as well make his next payment a little ahead of time while he had the chance and that I could mail a receipt to his New York address. Which I did. This was only a few days before the call came from Medfield so I was able to give the most recent date that he'd been in Hartford."

Miss Lazinski, all unknowing of what she had precipitated, spoke with modest pride of this display of efficiency.

The inspector didn't enlighten her on its consequences. He asked, "Did you keep the note?"

"I just dropped it in the wastebasket."

"When was the last time you saw Johnston?"

"The only time I ever saw him was the day he came to make his arrangements with me a year ago last January. He's been away——" She broke off. Put into words for the benefit of this quiet-voiced man whose dark eyes regarded her so thoughtfully, the whole thing had an improbable sound to Miss Lazinski herself. She reddened with embarrassment. What was the matter with her that she'd let it go on all this time, telling herself that it was Mr. Johnston's own affair if he wanted to keep on paying her good money when he got almost nothing in return?

Now she was mixed up in she didn't know what.

Madden turned a page in his notebook. "May I have a description of him, Miss Lazinski?"

"Well . . ." She dug into her memory for a description of a man she'd seen only once, briefly, over fourteen months ago. "He wasn't what I'd call tall——"

The inspector stood up. "As tall as I am?"

She measured his five eleven with her eye. "No, I wouldn't say so. Not nearly. It's hard to tell because he had a much heavier build. Maybe he was a little above average. Very dark hair, I remember. Almost black, I guess. Dark-rimmed glasses."

"About how old would you say he was?"

"Oh, I don't know. Perhaps forty."

"What color were his eyes?"

"Well . . . Dark as his hair, I think." She sounded doubtful. Her voice took on assurance as she added, "I remember what he wore. I didn't like his clothes. He had on a loud checked topcoat and a loud plaid suit under it. And a pink shirt. Imagine. A real bright pink, too. Personally, I like white shirts on men. And quiet clothes." Her glance conveyed approval of Madden's dark suit and tie and white shirt. "Mr. Johnston was what I'd call a real loud dresser. No taste at all, I thought."

Johnston's clothes had been intended to obscure the man.

"Any mannerisms or peculiarities you noticed?" he asked next.

"Not that I remember."

"Voice? Diction?"

She looked blank for a moment. Then she said, "Oh, you mean educated?"

"Yes."

"He talked all right, I guess. I didn't notice anything." Memory was at work. She added, "I think he had kind of a hoarse voice, though. As if he had a cold."

Pebbles, pellets of hard candy, or something of the sort in his mouth? Mrs. Meeker had also mentioned Johnston's hoarse voice, attributing it to the flu he was supposed to have.

"Do you think you'd recognize his voice again?"

"Oh no." She looked at Madden helplessly. "After all, just one conversation over a year ago—and so many strangers in and out of here since——"

"I know. You've done well to remember as much as you have. It's been very helpful."

"I feel so guilty," she said in a low voice. "I feel as if I've done something criminal myself. I should have known better. No calls on his phone, no mail to speak of, the way he steered clear of me——"

"Don't worry about it," Madden said. "If it hadn't been you, it would have been someone else. One more question: Did you do any typing for him the day he came here or any other time?"

"No, he never asked me to."

"Well, may I have a specimen from your machine anyway? Just in case something should come up." There was no point in alarming her with the possibility that Johnston had been getting into her office with a skeleton key and using her typewriter.

Miss Lazinski typed her name, address, occupation, and the

make and age of her electric typewriter on a sheet of paper and handed it to him. "Will this do?"

"Fine, thank you." Madden folded the sheet of paper and put it in his notebook.

He stood up to leave and gave her his card. "If you think of anything else, Miss Lazinski, or if you hear from Johnston by letter or phone, I'd like to have you get in touch with me." He smiled. "I don't mention your seeing him. I doubt that he'll show up here or that you'll ever hear from him again."

She walked to the door with the inspector and said anxiously, "I won't know what to do if he pays me again next month and sends the money for the phone bill."

"I wouldn't worry about it," Madden advised. "It's not going to happen. When the time is nearly up just call the telephone company and have the phone taken out."

"All right, if that's what you think." She sighed heavily. "From now on, anyone who wants mailing service will have to bring me a reference from the President of the United States and maybe Congress too."

Madden laughed. "Well, at least you've learned something from it."

"I certainly have, Inspector. My father and mother always said if money comes too easy you have to look at it twice to see if it's honest. They said you have to work for what you get in this world."

"Good advice, Miss Lazinski. I'll keep in touch with you. Thanks a lot."

He made his departure. Miss Lazinski watched him go. Visions of Johnston under arrest, a trial at which she would receive unfavorable publicity weighed on her as she returned to her desk. What would her father and mother say?

Back at his desk in Dunston, Madden compared the specimen from Miss Lazinski's typewriter with one of Johnston's letters to Mrs. Meeker—the other had been sent to the Bureau in Washington yesterday—and saw at once that the type was totally dissimilar; Johnston's letter had not been written on Miss Lazinski's typewriter.

It was midafternoon. Tad returned from his round of inquiries at Dunston banks. He'd had no luck, he said. None of the people on his list had accounts or safe-deposit boxes at any of them.

He could try Hartford banks next, Madden suggested, and, when Tad groaned, added unfeelingly, "Well, you wanted to be a postal inspector. You might as well find out early in the game how deadly dull the job can be. And if you have time while you're there, you could try his letter at a couple of the big printers—Johnston would seek the anonymity of a big one—just on the chance that he had his stationery printed in Hartford. Don't spend much time on it. Even if you hit the right place, probably all you'll get will be the date of the order. He'd have paid cash and picked it up himself."

"Okay. Tomorrow?"

"No, Friday. We're going to New York tomorrow. New lead on Johnston or another dead end."

Chapter Eleven

THEY made an early start the next morning. At nine-thirty they were in New York and left Madden's car in a parking lot within walking distance of Johnston's West Fifty-second Street address.

As Madden had feared, this turned out to be another dead end, the office of the Acme Mailing Service, located in a small brick building so old that it must soon become a victim of the city's ever-changing face.

It was a busy office. What information it could supply on Johnston came from its records. He had been a client since January 22, 1959, paying one month in advance on that date and arranging to have his mail held until called for. Thereafter he had made bimonthly payments in advance by money order. No one remembered anything about him. He phoned every two weeks or so to ask if he had mail and, if he had, sent a messenger to collect it. There was discussion as to what messenger service he had used; no one had paid much attention. He had no mail waiting to be collected at the present time.

City and telephone directories were available in the office. In no borough of the city was there a listing, alphabetical or classified, for Henry Johnston, insurance investigator.

Madden talked with the manager, explaining that Johnston was wanted for questioning in a fraud and murder case. Although he felt very sure that the mailing service would never hear from Johnston again, he suggested ways of trapping him if he should phone to inquire about mail.

From the mailing service office Madden and Tad went to the nearest branch office of the Motor Vehicle Department. There they learned that no Henry Johnston who might be their man had a New York driver's license or a car registered in his name.

They had spent a barren morning. After lunch they went back to Dunston.

The coroner's findings on Mrs. Meeker's death—suffocation brought about by the deliberate act of some person or persons unknown—returned the case to the first page of the newspapers the next morning.

Madden sent Tad to Hartford but had other cases that demanded his attention that day. He spent a large part of the morning with a psychiatrist and an assistant United States district attorney, conferring on a man about to go to trial on twelve counts of mailing obscene photographs. He had a record of four previous convictions on the same charge.

Most of the postal inspector's afternoon was given to the postponed chore of obtaining statements from three local victims of a nationwide work-at-home scheme based on the purchase of overpriced knitting machines.

He returned to his office just ahead of Tad, who came in and reported that his inquiries at Hartford banks had been as negative as those he had made in Dunston.

He had, however, without much trouble located the large printing company Johnston had gone to for his stationery. He had placed an order for one hundred letterheads with envelopes to match on May 12, 1959, and called for it on May 20, 1959. Payment had been made in cash; there was no record of a check. No one in the printing-company office remembered him. There had been no reorder.

"A lot of this thing seems to center on Hartford," Tad commented when he had made his report.

"And some of it on New York," Madden said. "Medfield is about halfway between the two—if that means anything."

That evening he took Tad to dinner at a friend's. Tad was so correct, so polite in his attentions to the twenty-year-old daughter of the house that Madden knew he wasn't interested and pondered anew the spark, the alchemy that attracted a man and woman to each other.

Whatever it was, he saw it at work the following Monday between Tad and Joan Sheldon. Glances, awareness of each other, tentative warmth were all apparent to Madden.

His mail that morning included a report from the Bureau in Washington on Johnston's handwriting. The specimens Madden had submitted had a common source, the report said, and appeared to be written with the off-hand rather than normal signatures.

"So now we know," Madden said. "Johnston is someone close enough to Mrs. Meeker or a member of her household to worry about his handwriting giving him away."

They went to Medfield, stopping first at the police station, where they found Pauling just back from a session with the Pecks and Joan Sheldon. They were still at Hilltop House, he said; it was being kept open until after appraisers were appointed and an appraisal made. He had questioned the Pecks and Joan for two solid hours, going over every incident of the night of Mrs. Meeker's death and events that had preceded it. He'd questioned Peck again about that long-ago prison record he had. He'd got from Joan Sheldon the names of two more men she had dated within the past year.

"She got real mad about it, too," he added. "Can't say I blame her. But if one of them's mixed up in the Johnston fraud he had a confederate sending in the reports. So I have to keep working on it. Johnston's the only good motive for the murder that I've got so far."

"They're all home now?" Madden inquired.

"They were when I left fifteen minutes ago. You want to see them about something?"

"Yes." Madden told the police chief what the report from Washington said. "I want specimens of their off-hand writing. And Thayer's. The lawyers' too."

"I've looked up their financial standings," Pauling said. "Hohlbein's solid as a rock. Garth has a fifteen-thousand-dollar mortgage on his house and a note for five thousand at the Medfield Trust Company. His father left plenty but the mother's still alive and there are four sisters, too. His father and Mr. Hohlbein were law partners as far back as I can remember."

"Ah," said Madden. "Then it wasn't ability alone that got our Mr. Garth where he is. Oh well . . . I'd better be on my way to Hilltop House to ruffle the ruffled feathers some more."

Pauling looked at his watch. "I'm due to start ruffling Thayer's in about ten minutes. He's coming in for another session with me. I'm thinking of sending a man to Philadelphia to do some firsthand checking on him and that car of his in the hotel garage."

"It is almost too good to be true," Madden agreed. "Have you had a look at his expense account yet? He travels around the country a lot."

"He has a flat annual allowance for expenses. Doesn't have to keep records that would show where he was at any particular time."

"What's his financial picture?"

"Good, but not good enough to account for the fraud money. Want me to try to keep him here for you?"

"If you can. May I use your phone to call Hohlbein and Garth?"

"Help yourself." Pauling pushed the instrument across the desk.

Both members of the firm were available today and would see him.

He stood up to go. Pauling leaned back in his chair and looked at him. "It seems to me they'd all be within their legal rights if they refused to give you specimens of their handwriting," he said.

"They won't," Madden assured him placidly. "Think what it would imply."

"Well, better luck than I had," Pauling said. "I'll try to keep Thayer on ice for you."

Messrs. Hohlbein and Garth were right-handed, they said. The postal inspector requested specimens of their normal signatures and left-hand writing for comparison with documents in his possession. It was a matter of elimination, he explained, and would be applied to all who had been associated with Mrs. Meeker.

Mr. Hohlbein agreed to the request with unmoved dignity and, when the younger partner began an indignant protest, quelled him with a glance. "I'm sure, William," he said, "we are prepared to do whatever we can to aid the inspector's investigation."

Did everyone call Garth William? Surely, Madden thought, some people called him Bill.

He brought out cards. Mr. Hohlbein wrote his name with his right hand in neat Spencerian script, shifted the pen to his left hand and wrote it again, and finally, at Madden's suggestion, wrote "Henry Johnston" beneath the two versions of his own signature. He held the pen very awkwardly in his left hand and wrote in a barely legible scrawl.

Garth followed his example in cold silence. His left-hand writing was no better than Mr. Hohlbein's.

It was Mr. Hohlbein who answered Madden's question about the money missing from Mrs. Meeker's Dunston bank account. No trace of it had been found, he said.

Madden's thank you included both of them. He made his departure.

He had left Tad waiting in his car while he was in the law office, but at Hilltop House he took the student inspector in with him.

Mrs. Peck answered the door. Hostility settled on her face when she saw who it was. Then, her voice tinged with resignation, she said, "Come in."

Madden asked if her husband and Miss Sheldon were home. "I'd like to see all of you," he said.

"I'll tell them." She left the two men standing in the hall while she went away to summon the others.

Joan Sheldon appeared first. She wore a gray wool dress with a full skirt and had her hair tied up in a pony tail. She said, "How do you do," on a formal note, but her glance went at once to Tad. Then she said, "Won't you come and sit down?" and led the way to the stiff, old-fashioned parlor familiar from their previous visit.

"Mr. Peck's outdoors somewhere," Joan said. "The ground's too damp to do much but I guess he wanted to get off by himself. The police chief was here earlier and upset him."

Her deep blue eyes were beautiful but always too serious when he saw her, Tad reflected. What were they like when she laughed? She looked about eighteen with her hair in a pony tail. It was impossible to associate her with Mrs. Meeker's murder.

She went on, her gaze fixed on Madden. "I feel sorry for

him. No one knew about the trouble he was in years ago until this happened. It's too bad it had to come out."

"It can't really hurt him as long as he had nothing to do with Mrs. Meeker's murder," Madden said.

"Of course he had nothing to do with it. He says it was a prowler, but I think it was Johnston; or perhaps it was Arthur Williams, whoever he is. It seems——" She stopped short. "That reminds me—Mr. Garth and I started going through Mrs. Meeker's papers this morning and came across some pictures I want to show you. I'll go get them."

She left the room and came back with two pictures. Tad, seated beside Madden on a sofa, caught the clean smell of her newly washed hair as she bent forward to hand the pictures to the postal inspector. Her glance met Tad's and she gave him a fleeting little smile.

"She really is a dish," he told himself, and then rejected the hackneyed phrase. "She's a darling, that's what she is. She had no more to do with Mrs. Meeker's death than I had. And as soon as this case is cleared up——"

He smiled back at her and made a ceremony of bringing out his pipe.

Madden looked at the two photographs. One of them, dark and mottled with age, showed a handsome young man not more than twenty. His haircut and middle part and high stiff collar dated the photograph back at least fifty years. "To Ada with love" was written at the bottom in faded ink, and in the lower right corner Clifton Studio, Somerville, Iowa, lettered in gold.

The second photograph was an unmounted modern print of a handsome young man, not more than twenty, with a crew cut, button-down shirt, and striped tie. Aside from these differences it might have been a photograph of the other young man. Feature for feature, eyes, mouth, high forehead, straight nose, the faces were identical.

Madden turned the print over. There was no negative number, nothing on the back to indicate where it had been taken or who had taken it.

Tad compared them. "They look like the same guy."

Madden shook his head. "Fifty years or so apart? The other one's an old man now if he's still alive."

"He isn't," Joan contributed. "It's Arthur Williams, Mrs. Meeker's old boy friend. He died a long time ago. They were never actually engaged but they'd talked of marriage. Then there was a quarrel or something and he moved to Texas with his family and they never saw each other again. But she kept his picture. Sometimes, she said, she wondered what her life would have been like if she'd married him. She told me quite a lot about him one night but I've forgotten most of it. It was almost two years ago."

"What about the modern picture?" Madden asked.

"I don't know a thing about it. I didn't know it existed until I came across it this morning. But just from looking at the two pictures, it must be the grandson of the other Arthur Williams. I never saw such a resemblance."

"Neither did I," Madden said. "May I borrow them? They'll get the best of care."

"Well . . ." She looked doubtful for a moment. "They're not mine. Still, I guess it's all right. You'll need a big envelope to put them in. I'll get you one."

She went out of the room and came back with an envelope.

"Thank you." The inspector put the pictures in it. They would be mailed to Washington right away. Already a thought about them had entered his mind.

The Pecks appeared in the doorway, she still hostile, Peck's narrow face wearing a suspicious scowl.

Madden and Tad stood up to greet them.

"Well, what is it this time?" Peck demanded, advancing into the room.

He needed smoothing down. Pauling must have been very rough on him, Madden thought, giving him a pleasant smile.

"Suppose we all sit down," he said, and waited until the Pecks, grudgingly, seated themselves. Then he continued, "I'm not having much luck finding Henry Johnston . . ."

The Pecks weren't interested, but Joan was as he talked a little about his efforts in this direction. Presently he showed them the cards Mrs. Meeker's lawyers had signed and brought out blank ones for their signatures. No suspicion was attached to anyone in particular, he explained. It was a question of eliminating them as authors of the Johnston signature. Were they right-handed or left-handed?

The Pecks would have balked, perhaps, at signing the cards, but Joan set them an example saying, "Yes, of course," as she took the card and pen the inspector proffered.

Her normal signature consisted of large, loosely joined letters. When she transferred the pen to her left hand her signature and the Henry Johnston she wrote beneath it were barely readable.

Watching her, Madden noticed that there was something wrong with the way she held the pen. Mr. Hohlbein and Garth had revealed the same kind of awkwardness, and he saw it again when the Pecks wrote on their cards, but he couldn't think what it was that puzzled him.

"What about Mr. Thayer?" Mrs. Peck asked as she handed back her card. "Are you going to get him to sign a card too?"

"Oh yes."

She looked mollified. The Pecks weren't being singled out for persecution because of Wilbur's prison record, which he hadn't seen fit to mention to her when he asked her to marry him twenty-five years ago.

She eyed her husband sourly. He was a slippery customer. A fool as well, being so quick to tell Pauling about his record. Afraid, he told her afterward, that his fingerprints would be taken, and thinking that it would be better to make the admission than to have the police find it out for themselves.

And then they hadn't had their fingerprints taken after all, Mrs. Peck reminded herself bitterly, not knowing that Pauling had used tact in getting them from objects handled. Wilbur had made his admission for nothing and was now regarded with suspicion by the police. But he hadn't killed Mrs. Meeker. She'd lived with him long enough to know that he hadn't done it. Besides, he wasn't smart enough to have thought up that business of Henry Johnston.

What about that brother of his, though, out in Racine? Or supposed to be in Racine. He was ten times as smart as Wilbur and mixed up in many a shady deal in his time.

This uneasy thought had been going in and out of Mrs. Peck's mind since she had first heard about Johnston.

Her husband hadn't revealed his brother's existence to the police. Neither had she. Nor did she intend to.

She watched Madden put the cards they had signed in his pocket. Wilbur signing things. She didn't like it.

"I should get back to Mrs. Meeker's papers," Joan remarked without moving.

"They'll keep," Tad said.

Mrs. Meeker's papers; all morning Mrs. Peck had been tempted to ask what the paper was that the Pecks had signed as witnesses last fall. But Joan had always been closemouthed about Mrs. Meeker's affairs. Mrs. Peck hadn't yet found the right moment to bring it up.

The doorbell rang. She went to answer it. Brian Thayer

was at the door. "Well, Mrs. Peck," he said. "Is the inspector here?"

"Yes." She stood aside to let him in and took satisfaction in adding, "He has something for you to sign."

She had never liked Brian Thayer.

He went ahead of her into the parlor. His manners were saved for people more important than the housekeeper.

He told Madden that he had an appointment a little later and thought it would save time to come here rather than wait at the police station.

"I won't keep you long," Madden said. He brought out a card and his fountain pen and explained what he wanted. Then he added, "I'm getting these signatures from everyone associated with Mrs. Meeker."

"It's nice to know I'm not being singled out for special favors," Thayer commented dryly.

He signed his name with his right hand and, after a moment's fumbling, with his left. He wrote "Henry Johnston" below his two signatures with his left hand and gave the card and pen back to Madden. "That's harder to do than you'd think," he said.

"Yes, it seems to be." Madden still didn't know what it was that puzzled him about the left-handed writing he had been watching.

Thayer had given Mrs. Peck her opening. She said, "It takes longer to write with the left hand, don't it, Mr. Thayer? You're a lot faster than I am, though, with your right hand. I noticed it last fall when Mrs. Meeker had us in to witness your signature to some paper."

She looked at him expectantly. Now, maybe, she'd find out what that paper was that they'd worried about at the time. They'd been silly, of course. A friend of Wilbur's had told them later on that they wouldn't have been called in as witnesses if it concerned some change, referring to them, in Mrs. Meeker's will. But she had behaved in a funny way as if she wasn't sure she was doing the right thing.

Thayer looked back at Mrs. Peck blankly. "I don't recall the paper. It must have had something to do with one of the scholarships."

"Oh." Mrs. Peck's expression conveyed doubt. "It was the only time we were ever——"

"Yes. But that's what it was." He was abrupt in dismissing the incident.

More abrupt than seemed necessary, Madden thought. And quick thereafter to leave.

The Pecks excused themselves. But Tad, the inspector noticed, was in no hurry, nor did Joan appear eager to speed his departure.

Chapter Twelve

MADDEN found an air-mail letter from a San Antonio inspector on his desk when they got back to the office. He read it aloud to Tad.

It began with the length of Johnston's stay in the city. The register of the hotel where he was supposed to have spent three weeks revealed that he had spent three nights there: August 5, August 6, and August 24. A bellboy admitted that in return for a generous tip he had secured blank billheads from the hotel office for Johnston on the assumption that he was going to chisel on his expense account. No car of his had been kept in the hotel garage, although Johnston had billed Mrs. Meeker for it. Airline manifests listed him on two flights to New York on the dates that he checked out of the hotel. He had not, during either stay, availed himself of the services of the public stenographer in the hotel. However, the San Antonio inspector had located one, name and address given, in the vicinity, to whom Johnston had dictated the first report sent from San Antonio. She remembered nothing about him. A carbon copy of the report in her files was all she had to go on.

The public stenographer to whom Johnston had dictated his second San Antonio report had been located a little farther removed from the hotel. She recalled that he had been in a hurry and had left a hotel bill to be enclosed when she signed and mailed the report.

The only obtainable description of him came from the bellboy who had supplied the blank billheads. He stated that Johnston was dark, rather stout, average height, wore dark-rimmed glasses, and was a flashy dresser.

A spot check by telephone of people mentioned in the reports had disclosed that they were bona fide residents of San Antonio, possibly taken at random from the telephone directory, since none of them had been interviewed by Johnston or had ever heard of the Williams family they were supposed to have known.

The San Antonio inspector said in conclusion that if the data already secured suggested any further line of inquiry to Madden he would be glad to be of service.

Enclosed were photostatic copies of the hotel register cards Johnston had signed.

Madden put down the letter. "So there it is," he said. "Good solid proof of the pudding. Pauling will want to hear about it. I'll have to give him a call."

"He rented a typewriter and typed up the hotel bills himself?"

"Yes. He could rent one at any railroad station or airport and Mrs. Meeker would not have know the difference between what a hotel issues and his phony bill."

"He flew back to New York both times. You said this thing centered on New York as well as Hartford."

"He'd change planes in New York anyway to get to Hartford." Madden reached for the phone. "We'll see what the manifests show at Bradley Field."

He made the call. Henry Johnston had not been a passenger out of Bradley Field on or within a reasonable margin of the dates Madden mentioned.

"So we're back at New York again," the inspector commented, and picked up the receiver to call the Medfield police chief. While he waited for the switchboard to put the call through he said, "As we get more reports in on Johnston they'll just repeat what we got from San Antonio. I doubt he ever put in an hour looking for Arthur Williams. In fact"—his dark brows came together in a frown—"I'm beginning to doubt that such a person exists. This whole damned case is like a set of children's boxes that fit one inside another; we have lies fitting inside each other ad infinitum."

He was connected with Pauling just then and gave him a résumé of the information from San Antonio. "We can talk it over tomorrow," he added. "I'll be in Medfield again."

He hung up and took out the pictures Joan had given him. "At least we know the first Arthur Williams actually existed," he said. "I'll get these off to Washington with the hotel signatures and ask to have the report on them expedited." He grinned. "They'll love me down there."

"We're going to Medfield tomorrow?" Tad inquired.

"In the afternoon. In the morning we'll inquire around the colored section and see if we can't locate a missing witness in the case of Clement Jones versus United States, which comes to trial"—he glanced at his desk calendar—"the day after tomorrow."

"Oh, the guy selling love philters through the mails."

"Yes, that one. Sexual prowess guaranteed."

Madden said next, "I want to talk to Joan Sheldon tomorrow about the paper Thayer signed with the Pecks as witnesses. Something about the attitude he took this afternoon made my hackles rise." Madden looked at his watch as he said this. "Say, it's almost quarter of six and here we are, good, apple-polishing little boys working overtime. Suppose we stop for a drink somewhere and have dinner together—or have you made other plans?"

"No, no plans at all."

"Not very enterprising for a young fellow, are you?" Madden queried. "I intend to go home myself after dinner and putter around with stamp albums. But I expected better things of you."

Tad, grinning noncommittally, said nothing.

They talked with Joan the next afternoon in her office across the hall from Mrs. Meeker's sitting room.

Madden led up to the subject he wanted to discuss. He said, "You told me, didn't you, that you had nothing to do with the scholarship fund in your job?"

She nodded. "It's entirely Brian Thayer's responsibility. Once I typed something Brian wanted Mrs. Meeker to sign in a hurry but that's the only work I ever did on it."

"Was it the paper Mrs. Peck mentioned witnessing yesterday?"

"No, it was just some form that had to be filled out and it was at least two years ago." She paused. "I was sort of surprised by what Mrs. Peck said. The first I'd heard of it." Her forehead creased in thought, Joan added, "It was all so routine, I can't imagine what Brian had to sign connected with the scholarships that would require two witnesses."

"Neither can I," Madden told her. "If there was anything, it would have to come up at a meeting of the trustees, I should think." He got to his feet and walked across the room and back. Hands in his pockets, he looked at her and made up his mind, once and for all, that she had played no part in the fraud case or the murder and could be trusted. He said, "I have a hunch that Thayer lied about it. Two witnesses to a signature spells a deed, a transfer of money or property, a note signed. In this case, something to do with money, I think. Money runs all through it. Maybe I'm reaching pretty far out into the blue, but I'm wondering if the paper has some bearing on the missing fifty thousand of Mrs. Meeker's."

Joan looked startled. She said, "Well, it's still unaccounted for. I've gone through all her files, too. Mr. Garth and I worked on them until nearly midnight last night. He and Mr. Hohlbein were hoping we'd come across a record of it but we didn't."

"These were personal papers—none pertaining to scholarships?"

"None. As I told you, they're Brian Thayer's responsibility." Joan came to a halt. Then she said, "I don't know whether I should mention this, but Mr. Hohlbein arranged for a special audit of the Meeker Fund last week to bring it up to the date of Mrs. Meeker's death. It's been completed and every cent accounted for. That's not where the fifty thousand went."

"Uh-huh." Madden checked the time. They'd left Dunston later than intended and he hadn't seen Pauling yet. He'd let Tad take over here. No doubt he and Joan Sheldon would enjoy it. He said, "Tad, I want to run down to the police station. If Miss Sheldon doesn't mind, I'd like you to stay here and go through some memory exercises with her."

He turned to Joan. "Did you keep an engagement book or memo calendar for Mrs. Meeker?"

"Oh yes, always."

"Still got last year's?"

"It's somewhere around." Her glance went to her desk. "Mrs. Meeker liked to be able to refer back to things."

"Well, will you get it out and go over it with Inspector Chandler? See what Mrs. Meeker had on her schedule around November 17 when she took the money out of the Dunston bank. Maybe it will jog your memory to check back on what she was doing."

"I don't know," Joan said, getting up and going to her desk. "I'll try it, though."

Madden left them and went to the police station.

He found Pauling in a disgruntled mood. He'd just had a call from the detective he'd sent to Philadelphia yesterday to look into Thayer's alibi for the night of Mrs. Meeker's murder. The detective said he'd found out nothing that cast doubt on it. Thayer's car had not been taken out of the hotel garage all that night; with assistance from the Philadelphia police the detective had been checking car rental agencies in Philadelphia and across the river in Camden without result. None had a record of a car rental that night to Thayer or Henry Johnston.

"So there it is," Pauling said at the end of his recital. "Unless he rented a car under a third name, Thayer is out of it."

"Whoever Johnston is, he probably does use a third name," Madden said. "He's been withdrawing Mrs. Meeker's money from his bank almost as fast as he put it in, which indicates a safe-deposit box somewhere. Or high living. I doubt that, though. He's been too careful all the way to make a splash with it."

"Unless Johnston has a partner we know nothing about," Pauling said. "If the money was turned over to him he could put it in the bank under his own name and we'd have no way to trace it."

The inspector shook his head. "I can't see that kind of a deal. They'd know there was always some chance of the thing blowing up in their faces and they'd want the money where they could get it in a hurry. I think it's in a safe-deposit box under a name that has no other connection with the case."

"You cheer me up," the police chief said. "You want me to start checking every safe-deposit box in the state of Connecticut?"

Madden smiled. "Well, there's always a crystal ball, isn't there?"

In the discussion that followed he didn't bring up the paper the Pecks had witnessed. He saw no point in mentioning a thing so lacking in substance.

An hour later he picked up Tad, who had no information for him. He had gone through last year's engagement book with Joan day by day from September to December 31 without coming upon anything that gave a clue to the missing money or the paper Thayer had signed. No appointments were listed for November 17, the day Mrs. Meeker drew the money out of the bank, and only routine ones for several days thereafter. Joan's memory had not been jogged by any of them.

"Too bad," Madden said, and added, tongue in cheek, "What I thought was a brain wave turned out to be just a waste of your time."

"No indeed," Tad declared briskly. "I made a little time on my own with Joan. First names now and all that."

"Well," said Madden. "Well . . ."

Chapter Thirteen

FEDERAL COURT appearances took up so much of Madden's time for the next two days that he had to wait until the new week had begun to return his attention to the Johnston fraud. In the meantime his request for assistance had brought in reports from inspectors in Houston and Santa Fe, Gary, Indiana, and Detroit. As Madden had predicted, they showed Johnston following his San Antonio procedure, billing Mrs. Meeker for days and weeks at hotels where he had made overnight stops; making up reports and dictating them to public stenographers but never signing them himself. Airline manifests listed him on three flights to New York and one to Chicago. The copy of a birth certificate sent from Houston and later disavowed turned out to be that of an Arthur Williams whose accidental death was reported in Houston newspapers on a date when Johnston had actually been in the city; he had taken advantage of the coincidence to lend an authentic touch to his Houston report.

In Santa Fe a clerk at the hotel where Johnston had stayed recalled that he had asked for a blank billhead to make a copy of his bill for his own records. No genuine search for Arthur Williams had been made in any city Johnston had visited. Over a month ago he had registered for one night at the Detroit hotel from which his last report had been sent. Wherever he stayed he gave his home address as Hartford, Connecticut. Copies of his hotel register cards revealed a signature that matched very closely those already in Madden's possession.

When the postal inspector was free to take up the case again, he sat down to talk it over with Tad. "From what we know now," he said, "I think we can label the grandson of Mrs. Meeker's old friend the Arthur Williams myth. She was sold quite a bill of goods on him."

"I don't follow you all the way on that," Tad said. "Just because Johnston didn't look for him——"

"He knew better."

"But he must exist somewhere. Johnston couldn't have made him up out of whole cloth. He'd be a young man—why couldn't he be in the armed forces or at school somewhere?"

"Not according to what Mrs. Meeker believed. Look at the way he was supposed to be moving around. A Ulysses in modern dress." Madden thought about it. "That's what makes the whole thing so preposterous. A fantasy. I want to know why she swallowed it, what made it even remotely plausible. It seems to me——"

His phone interrupted him. He picked up the receiver, said, "Madden," and then, "Oh, Miss Sheldon. Good morning. How are you? . . . You have?"

Tad saw a pleased look come to his face as he listened. Very faintly Tad could hear her voice. How did she look this morning? Was her hair pinned up or in a pony tail?

Madden said at the end, "Well, good for you, Miss Sheldon. We'll see what we can find out. Thank you very much for calling."

He hung up and regarded Tad with satisfaction. "She's been thinking about your session with her the other day. This morning she put on a blouse she bought at a sale in Dunston last fall and remembered that she was free to go shopping that day because Mrs. Meeker went to Bridgeport and didn't ask her to go along or tell her why she was going herself. It was an impromptu trip, which is the reason you didn't find it in the engagement book. Peck drove her. Miss Sheldon just asked him about it. He says she had him let her off at some restaurant downtown. She was going to have lunch and told him to pick her up there and to allow her about two hours because she had to go to a bank. He doesn't remember the name of the restaurant or just where it was."

"Banks again?" Tad looked pained.

"Yes. But limited. Mrs. Meeker would have gone to a good restaurant within walking distance of the bank she was headed for. She wouldn't walk far, either, with her arthritis."

"She could have taken a cab to the bank."

"I don't think so. If she'd intended to do that, she'd have told Peck to pick her up at the bank instead of going back to the restaurant."

"So all I have to do is find a good restaurant with a bank within stone's throw of it," Tad said resignedly.

"Yes. And while you're gone I'll tackle the paper work that's been piling up on me."

"I prefer banks, God-awful as they are," Tad said.

"So do I," Madden said.

He had to remind Tad to wear his hat.

Tad sighed, put it on, and left.

He came back in midafternoon wearing a grin of triumph as well as the despised hat.

Madden, still at his desk, looked up at him and said, "News?"

"Uh-huh. Second bank I went to, I hit the jackpot. Mrs. Meeker rented a safe-deposit box there November 18, 1959, the day after she drew the money out of the Dunston bank, and authorized access to the box for Thayer. She never went near it again herself but Thayer signed to get into it April 1 at two-ten P.M. He didn't lose much time going after the fifty thousand, did he? He must have headed straight for the bank the minute he could get away from Pauling. I wonder how he got hold of the key."

"That's only one of the questions we're going to ask him. But let's find out if he's home before we start for Medfield." Madden reached for the phone and put in a call to Brian Thayer. There was no answer. He hung up at last, thought a moment, and called Joan, who told him that Thayer was in Massachusetts, she didn't know just where, and wouldn't be back for a couple of days.

Madden and Tad were left eying each other with a sense of anticlimax.

Tad was the first to speak. "At least we've got time to think about the best way to tackle him. He'll lie like hell, I imagine."

"At the moment, we can't prove the money was ever in the box. And if we could get a court order to open it, we'd find it empty now."

"Could you even say he stole the money when she gave him access?" Tad asked.

"I don't suppose you could. But he signed something, some stipulation regarding its use, that the Pecks witnessed."

"Maybe the paper was in the box too," Tad suggested.

"With the money? That would be trusting Thayer a little too far."

"What about Mrs. Meeker's insurance friend? If she turned it over to him and he was Johnston's partner——"

"The insurance friend and the Arthur Williams myth." Madden sat in thought, rubbing his chin. Then he said, "The way my mind is running right now, I think I'll make my own trek to Philadelphia. I'll leave you to Inspector Palmisano's tender mercies, go home and do a little quick packing and get started."

"Wish you luck," Tad said. "Maybe you'll come back with Thayer's scalp."

"Who knows?"

Madden picked up the telephone and made a call to the
inspector in charge in Boston, asking permission to travel into
another division. This was granted; blanket permission to
travel wherever he needed to was granted, in view of the
seriousness of the case.

At nine o'clock that night he registered at the Putnam, a
first-class hotel, one of the largest in the city. He was given a
pleasant room on the fourth floor with a view of Independence Hall from the windows. After he had freshened up he
went back downstairs to the desk and asked to speak to one
of the security officers. The chief of the night staff, a former
police detective, was summoned and took him into his office.

When Madden brought up Thayer's name he shook his
head. "I'm afraid I'm not going to be able to help you much,"
he said. "The Philadelphia police sent a man around first and
then a Connecticut officer came down last week. They sent
us a picture of Thayer from Connecticut right after the murder. We've shown it around and checked on him all we could.
He had a single on the third floor. We know he registered before six because he made a long-distance call to Connecticut
around that time. He had dinner here; he signed for it in the
dining room. He had breakfast in the coffee shop a little after
six the next morning. Between dinner and breakfast all we
know is that he didn't go anywhere in his car. It was in the
hotel garage all night. No monkey business there with the
foolproof system we have for checking cars in and out."

"But Thayer himself wasn't seen around in the hotel after
dinner," Madden said.

"Not that anyone remembers. But what the hell"—the security officer shrugged—"an overnight guest in a big hotel
like this—who's to remember him three or four days later un-

less he got into some trouble or made a complaint that would impress him on the staff's mind?"

"Any other telephone calls?"

"Not unless he made them from one of the pay booths."

"He got an early start in the morning," Madden said next. "Did he leave word to be called?"

"No, he didn't."

"I wonder if he had a travel alarm clock," Madden mused aloud.

The security officer, big and solid in middle age, looked faintly troubled. "I'd have been better satisfied myself if we could have placed him here in the hotel between dinner and breakfast." After a pause he asked, "How far is it to the town in Connecticut where this murder took place?"

"About one hundred and eighty or ninety miles."

"Close to four hundred then to go there and back in one night."

"It could be done."

"Well, I'm afraid you can't prove it one way or the other by anyone here."

"Except that you offer assurance his car was absolutely inaccessible that night."

"Car rental agencies, of course," the security officer said. "He didn't rent one through us, though. We checked on it."

"He didn't rent one anywhere in Philadelphia under his own name or an alias we have in mind. Or in Camden."

"Plenty of suburban towns have car rental agencies. But where would you begin and end on a thing like that?"

"Distance would be a factor," Madden said.

"Yes, but you could spend a lot of time looking. In less than an hour out of here by train or bus a man could be in any number of places where he could rent a car. If you think Thayer's your man, though, I suppose it's worth it."

"I don't know if he is. I'm trying to find out."

The security officer eyed him with curiosity. "I didn't realize postal inspectors investigated murders. I thought it was out of their line."

"Well, when I'm investigating a fraud case and murder grows out of it, I don't retire to the side lines," Madden informed him.

"Oh, that's how it is."

"Yes. What time does the coffee shop open in the morning?"

"Six. The waitress who served Thayer will be on then. Ask for Beatrice. She remembered serving him, that he found fault with his eggs, but that was about all."

The security officer had nothing more to tell him. Madden thanked him and suggested a drink. He turned it down, explaining that he never took one while he was on duty. Madden went into the bar and had one himself, bought a magazine at a newsstand in the lobby, and went up to his room, leaving a call for six o'clock.

He had stopped in Medfield on his way to Philadelphia to get a picture of Thayer from Pauling and had it with him when he entered the coffee shop from the hotel lobby a little before six-thirty the next morning.

There were only two waitresses on duty at that hour, and a somnolent atmosphere prevailed in the long narrow room, which held only a few patrons eating early breakfasts. In another half hour it would begin to brighten up, the inspector thought, but for him it was a good time to ask questions.

The waitress who came to his table said that she was Beatrice. He ordered breakfast. No one else required her attention while it was being prepared.

Madden identified himself and brought out Thayer's picture. "Mr. O'Brien"—that was the security officer's name—

"says you were asked about this man a few days after he stayed at the hotel."

She looked at the picture. "Yes, I remember. He had breakfast here, I told them. He rubbed me the wrong way. He said he ordered four-minute eggs and his hadn't been cooked that long. When I offered to take them back, he said never mind, he was in a hurry."

Her tone was resentful. "He acted like it was my fault, like I'd cooked the eggs myself. Then he left me a measly dime for a tip. I didn't know whether it was to pay me back for the eggs or because he was just a cheapskate. You'd be surprised, the way some people——" She stopped short as it dawned on her that her remarks were less than tactful to a patron who hadn't yet had breakfast or tipped her.

The inspector filled in her awkward little pause. "What time did he come in here that morning?"

"No time after we opened. Maybe five after six." She turned away. "I guess your bacon and eggs are ready."

She was gone for two or three minutes. But apparently her thoughts were still on Brian Thayer. Setting Madden's order in front of him, she said, "You'd think I was the dirt under his feet. So fussy about his eggs but not so fussy about himself. Yesterday's shirt and needed a shave, too. I tell you, we get all kinds."

Madden smiled. "I guess you do."

She left him to his breakfast. While he ate he turned over in his mind what she had told him.

Thayer had made a fuss about his eggs but hadn't wanted to wait the extra few minutes to have others cooked to suit him. This could have been meaningless or it could have been intended to draw the waitress's attention to his presence at the hotel at an early hour of the morning.

Yesterday's shirt and Thayer's lack of a shave seemed more

significant to Madden. A man getting up in a hotel room to make an early start on a trip did what Madden himself had done that morning. He shaved and put on a clean shirt when he got dressed. These were things he did automatically unless he was a slob. Thayer had looked well groomed both times that Madden saw him. He didn't seem the type to go down to breakfast in a first-class hotel unshaven and wearing yesterday's shirt. But if he hadn't been in bed, if he'd spent the night driving to Medfield to kill Mrs. Meeker and back to Philadelphia to establish an alibi, he'd have looked no better than he did when the waitress saw him.

In Thayer's place, the inspector's thoughts continued, he wouldn't have risked going up to his room at six in the morning to shave and clean up. A less conspicuous arrival could be made through the coffee shop entering it from the street and half an hour later, after breakfast, appearing in the lobby and asking at the desk to have the bill made out and the car brought around from the garage. Then he could go up to his room for a quick shave and change of clothes and muss up the bed to look as if he'd slept in it.

This was theory. Proving it, Madden thought, was something else. If it was true, Thayer had rented a car. Not in Philadelphia, though, unless under an unknown name. Outlying town?

Let it go for the moment, Madden thought, smoking a cigarette with his coffee. He had better lines of inquiry to follow. He'd go back to Dunston.

He was careful to leave a generous tip for the waitress. On the way out he stopped to ask her if she'd noticed whether Thayer came into the coffee shop from the lobby or the street.

She hadn't noticed. He thanked her and left.

Chapter Fourteen

THE inspector was back in Dunston by eleven o'clock. Before he went to his office he stopped at police head-quarters with Thayer's picture. A police artist listened to his description of Henry Johnston and said that he would try his hand at darkening the hair and adding dark-rimmed glasses to the picture. Not that Madden hoped for much from it, but he could at least show it to Miss Lazinski and see what she said about it.

At the office he found in his mail a report on Johnston from Amarillo, Texas. It revealed the familiar pattern of the fraud but on the hotel register card enclosed Johnston's signature looked very different from the others Madden had obtained.

He compared it with one of them and said to Tad, who was looking on, "I think he slipped. Had an absent-minded moment and gave us a specimen of his normal handwriting."

"The criminal," Tad stated unctuously, "always makes a mistake."

"This one's made damned few," Madden reminded him. He sat looking at the two different signatures. Then he said, "I think we'd better get some more specimens of Thayer's writing to send to the Bureau with this Amarillo signature. Try Miss Sheldon. If she can't help you, see what the police chief has."

Tad had no complaints to make about this assignment. But when he was ready to leave he turned to Madden a little hesitantly. "Is it all right if I ask Joan out to dinner? Considering the case and all, I mean."

"Sure it is, as long as you keep it social. Let her talk but you say nothing."

"Sounds one-sided."

"Ours is a one-sided business." Madden smiled at him. "She isn't involved, Tad. She's a nice girl."

Tad beamed. "Isn't she, though?"

He came back from Medfield later in the afternoon with several specimens of Thayer's handwriting from Mrs. Meeker's files.

"Well, you had success," Madden greeted him, and added after a pause, "On both counts?"

"Both counts," said Tad. "Got a dinner date with her tonight."

He sat down with Madden and dutifully noted resemblances between Thayer's writing and Johnston's Amarillo signature but had a faraway look in his eyes most of the time, Madden thought.

He sent the new specimens to Washington before the day ended. They crossed in the mail a report from the Bureau on the handwriting specimens of all those on his first list of suspects in Medfield. They were negative except for Thayer's. Comparing his left-hand and normal signatures with Johnston's, the report said, "Notwithstanding differences in style which could be due to disguise or ambidexterity, certain agreements are observed which remotely suggest common authorship."

After Madden read the report he put in a call to Thayer. He was back from his Massachusetts trip and answered the phone. He seemed perfectly at ease when Madden said that there was something else he'd like to discuss with him. He would be tied up until about the middle of the afternoon, he said, but would be free from then on if Madden cared to come out.

They made an appointment for three o'clock.

This gave the inspector time to go to Hartford first. Accompanied by Tad, he went to Dunston police headquarters, picked up the retouched picture of Thayer, and took it to Hartford to show Miss Lazinski.

It was just as well he wasn't hoping for much from it. Miss Lazinski studied it conscientiously and then said on a helpless note, "I don't know what to tell you. It looks something like him. But I only saw him once, you know, over a year ago."

"Would you come out to Medfield and take a look at this man in the flesh?" Madden inquired. "He doesn't wear glasses or flashy clothes and his hair is quite light but still, seeing him might mean more than looking at his picture."

Miss Lazinski was ready to co-operate. She would close her office a little early and drive out to Medfield. She didn't know the town but could certainly find the post office, where they would meet her out in front at five-thirty.

Again, Madden had little hope. Miss Lazinski, he thought, lacked imagination. When she saw Thayer, sandy-haired, not wearing glasses or flashy clothes, he doubted that she would be able to relate him in any way to the man who had become her client fifteen months ago.

He would have to try, though. He had no one else who remembered Johnston's appearance at all.

The first thing Madden noticed about Brian Thayer when he admitted them to his apartment that afternoon was his good grooming. He wore a tweed jacket, slacks, and cordovans that looked expensive and well cared for. His shirt was immaculate, his hair neatly brushed, and he had shaved recently.

When they were seated in his office, he said that he'd got back from Massachusetts late last night, and went on to talk wryly of the difficulties of a Meeker scholarship recipient at M.I.T. who was in grave danger of flunking out and thus becoming one of the very few under their program to whom this had ever happened.

Madden and Tad listened with polite attention until Thayer cut himself short and said, "But it's my problem. What can I do for you, Inspector?"

He seemed just as much at ease now as earlier on the phone; a man with nothing on his conscience.

With no particular emphasis Madden replied, "You can tell me about the safe-deposit box Mrs. Meeker rented in Bridgeport last fall and gave you access to."

There was a pause during which Thayer swung his foot back and forth and looked at it with a troubled grimace as if it somehow displeased him. "Oh yes, that," he said at last, and gave Madden a slight, apologetic smile. "A foible of Mrs. Meeker's. I should probably have mentioned it and not left you to find it out for yourself."

He had been ready for the question; had always been ready for it from the day he opened the box. Madden didn't return his smile. He said, "Yes, you should have."

"It seemed like a private matter, though," Thayer continued. "That's the way I've thought of it since Mrs. Meeker broached it to me last fall. She had some papers, she said, that she wanted to keep as long as she lived but didn't want to have fall into her lawyers' hands after she was gone. She said that for the time being she would rent a box in a Bridgeport bank, put the papers in it, make me her deputy and turn the key over to me. Then, if she died without having done anything else about them, I was to go to the bank immediately after her death and destroy the papers unread. This I agreed to do. . . ."

He must have rehearsed the story many times, he told it so smoothly.

"Naturally, I thought of the box, as soon as I learned she was dead," Thayer continued. "But in spite of all the police activity that morning, I still felt that she was entitled to the privacy she had asked for. I had it in mind, of course, that if she hadn't died a natural death and the papers seemed to have the least bearing on it, I would turn them over to you or Mr. Pauling."

"You lost no time getting to the bank," Madden observed, his tone as smooth as Thayer's. "You showed foresight, too. You were there, weren't you, before her death came out in the newspapers? I believe it's Connecticut law that a safe-deposit box can't be opened by a deputy after the death of the box holder."

"Oh? I didn't know that. I don't suppose Mrs. Meeker did either. But she had laid a charge on me. I felt I should take care of it immediately. That's why I went to Bridgeport the moment Mr. Pauling finished questioning me."

"And found nothing, of course, that had to do with Mrs. Meeker's murder in the box." Madden permitted himself sarcasm. "Old love letters, perhaps?"

"Why, how'd you guess?" Thayer was earnest in surprise. "Five of them sealed up in a manila envelope. Under the circumstances, I didn't feel I could destroy them unread as she'd asked me to. I glanced through them just to see what they were."

"From Arthur Williams, no doubt?"

"Yes. There was nothing else in the box. It's empty now."

Madden refrained from saying, No fifty thousand dollars?

It would be a futile outlet for irritation when he couldn't prove that the money had ever been in the box.

"I destroyed the letters," Thayer added. "They had no connection with her death."

"Chief Pauling won't be any happier than I am when he hears about it."

Thayer shrugged. "Mrs. Meeker was entitled to respect for her wishes, however eccentric they seem to you."

"They seem unbelievably eccentric to me," Madden informed him coldly. "They will to Pauling. He's not going to like it, either, that you didn't mention the box to him." Madden's voice turned colder. "There's only your word for it that there were love letters in the box."

Thayer looked chagrined. "I hadn't thought of that. I'll have to tell him what I've just told you. I hope my reputation is solid enough for him to take my word on what I found and that it didn't seem important enough to mention."

Madden got to his feet. He'd had enough. He said, "Law enforcement officers take no one's word for anything, Mr. Thayer. They look for proof."

For the first time Brian Thayer seemed nonplused.

Back in Madden's car Tad said, "Neat and slick. Had his story all ready. He's a guy who plans every move ahead."

"He sure does." Madden headed for the post office. "I'm going to put a cover on his mail; see what we get from it."

"A confederate?"

"I don't know."

From the post office they went to the police station, where Madden brought the police chief up to date on what he had been doing for the past few days.

Pauling looked thoughtful over the report on Thayer's handwriting from Washington and what the waitress in the

Putnam Hotel had said and grim over the safe-deposit box in Bridgeport.

"By God, I'll have plenty to say to Thayer about that," he declared. "Love letters! What does he take us for?"

"The trouble is, you can't prove it wasn't love letters," the inspector pointed out.

"No, but maybe I can prove something else. I'll try hard enough, anyway."

Pauling summoned a subordinate and told him to get hold of a map of Philadelphia and its suburbs. "I'll send a man back there," he said. "If Thayer rented a car in any of the suburban areas I'm going to track it down."

Madden offered no opinion on how long it might take. "You might as well check the Philadelphia airport, too," he suggested. "He could have flown to New York and rented a car at LaGuardia if there was a flight back to Philadelphia that would get him there in time to hang on to his alibi at the hotel."

But it was too easy, Madden thought, even as he was making the suggestion. Johnston, whoever he was, Thayer or Thayer's confederate, had been too foresighted all along to leave an open trail at the Philadelphia airport.

At five-thirty they met Miss Lazinski in front of the Medfield post office and drove to Thayer's apartment, parking near enough to keep a watch on the front entrance. If he didn't go out to dinner, Madden would have to devise a plan to bring him out of the building.

Miss Lazinski was left alone in the front seat of her car, with Madden and Tad in back ready to duck down out of sight if it seemed necessary.

Shortly after six o'clock Thayer came out the front entrance. She had a good look at him as he crossed the street to his car. They followed him to a restaurant and she had a second look when he went inside. He wore no hat to hamper her view of him, but she wasn't sure. She made a valiant mental effort to put glasses on him and darken his hair, but she still wasn't sure, one way or the other. "His clothes are so different," she said. "And I remember Mr. Johnston as a shorter, heavier man."

Against his better judgment Madden pressed her a little. "Shoulders can be padded," he said. "So can a waistline."

Miss Lazinski shook her head unhappily. "I just don't know," she said.

That ended in defeat a day that had promised more than it had produced.

Chapter Fifteen

THERE was now a lull in the case, typical of investigative work, while the postal inspector, giving most of his time to other cases, waited to hear more from Washington.

While he waited, he queried the Bronx bank on the Johnston account and was informed that the balance remained untouched. The Hartford Post Office reported that Johnston had received nothing but junk mail. The letter carrier on Thayer's route knew nothing to his discredit; his mail, in the first few days after Madden put a cover on it, consisted only of routine bills and business correspondence.

The following Monday, Pauling phoned. Thayer, he said, couldn't be shaken in his story about love letters in the safe-deposit box. He'd gone to Bridgeport with the police chief, opened the empty box in his presence, and turned the key over to him. Pauling had informed an official of Mrs. Meeker's death, which hadn't come to the bank's attention. This was locking the barn door, he interjected, and went on to say that there was no listing for Thayer or Johnston at the Philadelphia airport the night of Mrs. Meeker's death; in any event, flight schedules ruled out the possibility that Thayer had flown to New York, rented a car, driven to Connecticut, and flown back to Philadelphia by six o'clock the next morning.

Train and bus schedules had been considered and ruled out, Pauling added. The man he had sent back to Philadelphia was now concentrating on suburban car rental agencies. He might have better luck with them.

Or none at all, Madden thought. How long did agencies keep records of car rentals?

"I sent a man to Red Bank, Thayer's home town, today," Pauling continued. "I want him checked back to his cradle."

"Let's hope he doesn't get wind of it," Madden said. "We wouldn't want him to cut and run before we get him pinned down."

"If your Washington lab says Thayer's right-hand signature and the one Johnston slipped up on in Amarillo are the same——"

"It's not always that definite when there's just a signature to go on."

The police chief felt out of his depth. "Then what good will it do?" he asked.

"If they say common authorship it will be conclusive as far as I'm concerned. I'll go after Thayer then for all I'm worth."

The report Madden was waiting for arrived in the next day's mail. There were, it said, definite suggestions of common authorship in Thayer's normal signature and the Johnston signature from Amarillo.

"How are you going to handle it?" Tad asked.

"I want to think about it," Madden said. "He's tough. He's had both Pauling and me on his neck without turning a hair. Next time I go near him I want to be in a position to nail him to the wall."

"If Pauling doesn't nail him first on a car rental," Tad said.

Madden raised a dark eyebrow in mock reproof. "There's no rivalry between law enforcement agencies. There is only co-operation. Hasn't that come up in one of your manuals, Tad?"

Tad grinned. "I seem to have read it somewhere. Conduct becoming to a postal inspector does not include glory-seeking or headline-hunting."

"You may go to the head of the class," said Madden.

His next report from Washington arrived the same day in the noon mail and referred to the pictures Madden had submitted of the first Arthur Williams and his modern twin. It stated that Photograph No. 1—the inspector had numbered them—was not of recent origin; that pictures changed and darkened with age and various mottlings and imperfections appeared in them. These changes had taken place in Photograph No. 1, supporting the conclusion that it dated back to the turn of the century as the clothing and hair style of the subject indicated.

Photograph No. 2, the report continued, appeared to be of very recent origin, but on the face alone, under a microscope, the pin-point mottlings and imperfections observed on the face in Photograph No. 1 were exactly duplicated. In view of this fact, Photograph No. 2 must be regarded as a composite photograph, made from the face of Photograph No. 1 and the head and shoulders of another subject.

"So that's how Thayer worked it," Madden said when Tad had read the report. "Clever. He produced the faked picture, let her draw her own conclusions from it and the stage was set for the Johnston fraud."

"It's a little puff for your ego," Tad commented. "You've been saying all along that Arthur Williams was a myth."

"Well, yes, he was, as the grandson of Mrs. Meeker's old friend. But another Arthur Williams or someone using the name enters the case somewhere. The fraud was based on him." Madden leaned back in his chair and considered the problem. Then he said, "Let's go see Miss Sheldon. Notice how formal I am, not calling her Joan. But then, I haven't your advantage of youth and I haven't improved shining hours with her——"

Tad's face turned red. Madden dropped his teasing and

said, "Maybe she can tell us where Mrs. Meeker kept Arthur Williams's picture. I'd like to know what chance Thayer had to get at it."

He phoned Joan first to make sure of finding her home. But when they arrived and rang the bell, she let Mrs. Peck answer the door. She wasn't going to be found waiting on the doorstep, in case Tad Chandler thought—— Well, that was silly of her when it was a business call. But just the same . . .

She waited in her office until Mrs. Peck summoned her.

Mrs. Peck was less wary of the postal inspector today. Pauling had been at the house yesterday, but the questions he asked were about Brian Thayer. She felt that it was safe to stop worrying about her husband's prison record and his ne'er-do-well brother in Wisconsin.

She was, for the first time, almost cordial in greeting Madden and Tad.

Joan took them into her office. She still felt silly over not answering the door herself and was prepared to be as helpful as she could to make up for it. She gave Tad a warm smile as he sat down near her.

Madden leaned on the back of a lounge chair. "I'm interested in the Arthur Williams picture, Miss Sheldon. Do you know where Mrs. Meeker kept it?"

"Oh yes. In the bottom drawer of her desk. We were in her sitting room the night she talked to me about him and she had me get it out."

"And after you'd looked at it, you put it back where it was?"

"Yes. She kept it under a folder of newspaper clippings on Mr. Meeker. And that's where I found it when I went through her desk after she died. The modern picture I gave you was clipped to it as if she'd been comparing them. No wonder. The resemblance was uncanny."

Madden shook his head. "Not at all, Miss Sheldon. Simple

trickery. The face of the original had a modern head and shoulders added to it. But keep this to yourself, please. I'm telling you about it to see if you can help us figure out when and how it was managed. The Williams picture had to be borrowed and photographed, you know. The composite was made from a photograph of the original picture."

Joan's deep blue eyes mirrored her astonishment. He gave her a moment to absorb what he had said. Then he asked, "Does Thayer have a camera? Make a hobby of photography?"

"Not that I know of. At least, he's never mentioned it to me."

"He would have if he made a hobby of it," Madden said. "And showed you pictures he took, too."

She smiled. "That's right. I know some amateur photographers." Her smile died. A shocked look supplanted it. She said, "But—— Surely you don't think that Brian——"

"I know he played the part of Johnston," Madden informed her. "I don't know if he murdered Mrs. Meeker. But wouldn't you say the two go hand in hand?"

Joan's face went white. "I can't believe it. It's horrible. Someone I've known for years—so controlled, even-tempered——"

"It wasn't a crime of passion. It was cold-blooded murder."

Joan was silent, looking off into the distance. After an interval she said slowly, thinking aloud, "Cold-blooded and coldhearted go together, don't they? I guess I've always thought Brian had a cold heart. He wasn't anyone you'd fall into a comfortable friendship with. Mrs. Meeker would talk sometimes about how capable and intelligent he was, and what a good administrator, but I don't think she ever really felt at all close to him." She paused, assembling her thoughts. "For all her arrogance, she had warmth, you know. Once she told me Brian was too machinelike for her taste; utterly honest and trustworthy but not a person she could warm to."

Biding his time for years? Madden wondered. Waiting to snatch at opportunity when it finally presented itself?

Joan went on in a small voice, "They still electrocute people for murder in this state."

"Not too often nowadays," Madden said.

Tad added reassurance. He said, "From what I've read in the papers since I came to Connecticut, a murderer can live out his normal life span on appeals in the state prison."

"Even so——" Joan shivered. Then she said, "But I should save my sympathy for Mrs. Meeker. Her murder was brutal. She had no chance at all. I can't think of anything worse than being smothered."

"It must have been quick, though, at her age," Madden said. "She couldn't have put up too much of a struggle. Anyway, it's over and done with for her. It's Thayer we have to think about. He defrauded her and probably killed her, too."

"Yes." Joan's color began to come back. "I wish it was all over, though, and this house closed and put up for sale or whatever . . . Would you care for a drink? I think I could do with one."

She needed it, Madden thought. "I'll have a light scotch and soda," he said. "How about you, Tad?"

"I'll have the same." Tad stood up. "May I help, Joan?"

"Well, the liquor cabinet's in the dining room."

They left the room together. By the time they came back with the drinks Joan seemed calmer and was even able to laugh at something Tad said to her.

Presently Madden turned the conversation back to the Arthur Williams picture. Mrs. Meeker, Joan said, hadn't shown it to Thayer in her presence and had never mentioned showing it to him at all. The modern composite had been kept entirely from Joan.

"She was secretive about lots of things," the girl added. "Suspicious that people were trying to pry into her affairs. She kept so much from me that I'm not surprised she didn't show me the other picture."

"And yet she showed you her picture of Arthur Williams," Madden commented.

"That was because she was in a reminiscent mood at the time. Perhaps if she'd lived, there'd have been a moment when she was in the mood to show me the other one. Although I was out of favor the last months of her life, you know."

"Did she keep the original picture in a locked drawer?"

"No, that drawer was never locked."

Madden felt that he had it all fairly clear now. Mrs. Meeker, in another moment of sentiment, had shown Arthur Williams's picture to Thayer. Perhaps, as with Joan, she'd had him get it out of the drawer for her and replace it; or at least she'd taken it out in his presence. Thayer had got hold of the picture at some later date when he was alone in the room and taken it away with him. There was little chance that Mrs. Meeker would miss it; he'd only have kept it long enough to have a copy of it made.

Not by a Medfield photographer, though, Madden's thoughts continued. Possibly someone in Dunston. When it came to having the composite made, Thayer had probably gone even farther afield. With the amount of traveling he did, it might have been made anywhere; he'd tell the photographer it was part of a joke. Hopeless to try to trace it without an identifying mark of any kind.

Once he showed it to her, Mrs. Meeker had been a sitting duck for the fraud Thayer had worked out.

Madden emerged from his thoughts to inquire of Joan, "Does Thayer have a key to this house?"

She shook her head. "No reason he should have."

"What were his chances of getting hold of one long enough to have a duplicate made?"

"Well . . ." Joan hesitated. "I'm sure he couldn't have got hold of mine. Probably not the Pecks', either. But Mrs. Meeker kept extra house keys around. They were supposed to be locked up——"

"She was apt to mislay them?"

"Sometimes. Especially after she began to have forgetful moments."

Thayer had been able to get hold of a key.

Joan betrayed nervousness by twisting a loose strand of hair around and around her finger. "If it was Brian—and he had his own key that night——"

"He may have had it for years, not knowing when he'd find a use for it."

She divided a troubled glance between Madden and Tad. "Then he left the door unlocked on purpose to make it seem Mrs. Peck or I forgot it?"

"Yes." After a pause the inspector added, "He hoped Mrs. Meeker's death would pass for a natural one. If it did, the unlocked door wouldn't be noticed; but if the question of murder came up, it was meant to confuse the issue by bringing an outsider, possibly a prowler into it."

Joan closed her eyes for a moment. "It sounds so dreadfully calculating and foresighted."

"It was. Months of planning went into the fraud. The murder was carefully planned too, even with very little time available for it."

"Who was Mrs. Meeker's insurance friend?"

"I have no idea."

Joan signed uneasily. "I'll be so glad when it's all settled one way or another," she said. "I wish I never had to lay eyes on Brian again. At least he doesn't have much reason to come here any more. I'll just stay out of his way when he does."

"But if you do run into him," Tad said, "try to act as if nothing's the matter."

"Yes, do," Madden said. Then he asked, "Have the trustees of the scholarship fund held a meeting since Mrs. Meeker's death?"

Joan nodded. "Yes, last week. But not here as they used to. The meeting was at Dr. Greer's. It was in the paper. Mr. Prescott, a businessman here in town, was appointed to the board to take Mrs. Meeker's place and Dr. Greer was elected chairman. I guess I've told you that Mr. Weltner—he and Dr. Greer are both retired—is the third trustee."

"Well, Mr. Prescott is brand new, but may I have the addresses and phone numbers of the others?" Madden took out his notebook.

Joan read them off from the telephone directory and then said, "I understand that Dr. and Mrs. Greer are going to Colorado to visit their married daughter. They may have left already."

"Oh," said Madden. "Then I'd better not lose time calling him. May I use your phone?"

Joan handed it to him across the desk. He dialed Dr. Greer's number first. There was no answer. When he tried Mr. Weltner's he had better luck. Mr. Weltner was home and would see him.

He and Tad said good-by to Joan and went to call on Mr. Weltner.

He came to the door himself and took them into his living room. Bald and spare, vague of eye and tone, he was all of Mrs. Meeker's age or older, Madden thought, and just as close to senility. It was to be hoped that the new trustee brought younger blood to the board.

Madden was purposeful now in his search for a young man who went by the name of Arthur Williams, whether it was rightfully his or not. He could dismiss from his mind once and for all the Texas-grandson myth and Thayer's insistence that no one of that name had ever applied for a Meeker scholarship.

At first it seemed that Mr. Weltner would be of no help. He didn't recall an Arthur Williams among the scholarship applicants last year. Then he said that he didn't think he had attended the meeting at which the recipients were selected. He rather thought that he was still in Florida when it was held, recuperating from a gall-bladder operation. He suggested they see Brian Thayer. He was a very competent fellow and would have all that information right at his finger tips.

Madden thanked him and decided against asking that he keep their visit from Thayer. As long as nothing was said to fix it in Mr. Weltner's mind it would probably slip right out of it.

He walked to the door with them, switching from praise of Brian Thayer to stressing the high caliber of the scholarship recipients. "Just last week," he said, "when we were briefing Prescott, the new trustee, Dr. Greer brought it up that over seventy per cent of our boys are elected to the National Honor Society. Remarkable potential showing up while they're still in high school, you see. As I told Prescott, educating boys like that is one of the most useful things that could possibly be done with Ulysses' money. He was a self-made man, you know. They don't make them like him any more. Whole world's changed, of course."

Mr. Weltner had, after all, made their visit to him worth while.

On the way back to the car Madden asked, "Do you know where the National Honor Society has its headquarters, Tad?"

"Washington, I should think," Tad replied. "Never made it myself."

"I'll get the address in Dunston. The superintendent of schools must have it."

During the drive back to Dunston, Tad turned the subject over in his mind and said, "There's the national association for scholarships at Princeton. Sort of a clearinghouse. It might offer another approach to the elusive Mr. Williams. If he did apply for a Meeker scholarship, he was an orphan to begin with, which could mean that he wouldn't be able to go to college without financial help. If that were the case, he certainly wouldn't limit himself to applying for a Meeker scholarship, would he? He'd want to have several irons in the fire and the association at Princeton could easily be one of them."

"Good point," Madden said.

"I should have thought of it long ago. And here's something else I should have thought of. If Williams wanted to go to college he took college boards." Tad paused. "How many colleges do you suppose there are in the country?"

"God knows," Madden said. "I just hope I don't have to find out."

Chapter Sixteen

IT was after five, too late to call the superintendent of schools, when they got back to Dunston that afternoon. The next morning the superintendent's office supplied the addresses Madden wanted.

The National Merit Scholarship Association in Princeton was within one day's journey. He would go there today. If it had no record of Arthur Williams, it could at least unravel the intricacies of college board examinations as a means of tracking him down, Madden thought.

Before he left, he dictated two letters. One would go to the National Education Association, asking if anyone named Arthur Williams, address unknown, had been elected to membership in the National Honor Society within the past three or four years. The other letter was to Dr. Greer at his forwarding address in Boulder, Colorado, given over the phone by the Medfield postmaster. Dr. Greer was asked if he recalled an applicant named Arthur Williams being considered for a Meeker scholarship last year, and a self-addressed, prepaid envelope was enclosed with a request for an early, airmail reply.

By midmorning the inspector was on his way to Princeton, leaving Tad to go out with a station examiner to audit one of the station accounts. He had a successful trip, but it was too late that night when he got back to call Tad about it.

Tad was in ahead of him when he reached his office the next morning. He saw that Madden had a pleased look on his dark face and said, "The cat that ate the canary. It paid off?"

"It sure did. It was a bright idea you had, Mr. Chandler. Arthur Williams, age eighteen, orphan, of Cleveland, Ohio, took the examination a year ago last fall for a merit scholarship, passed with a very high rating and on the basis of need was granted a full scholarship to Clarkson College, Potsdam, New York, which he entered last September."

Madden sat down at his desk. "I'm going to call Clarkson, make sure Williams is available and if he is, I'm on my way."

"You're not going to try to talk to him on the phone?"

"No indeed. For all I know, he's mixed up in the fraud. I want him right in front of me when I start asking questions. I should be able to handle a kid. I've had enough of a runaround from Thayer."

He picked up the telephone receiver.

He was put through to the college office. Arthur Williams, he was told, was still enrolled at the college and would probably be free in the early evening.

An hour later Madden was on his way to Potsdam. He drove to Massachusetts and took the turnpike that fed him into the New York Thruway. He made a brief stop on it for a late lunch and gas. After he left it for a two-way road, he laid out his map on the seat beside him and continued to make good time through the sparsely settled region of northern New York State.

At quarter of seven he was turning onto the college campus at Potsdam and at seven o'clock he was shaking hands with his quarry in a lounge. Arthur Williams, tall and gangly, had a prominent Adam's apple and an open smile on an engagingly artless face. He did not in the least resemble Mrs. Meeker's Arthur Williams.

Madden handed him his identification folder and said, "I've

made a special trip from Dunston, Connecticut, to see you, Arthur."

"Oh." Arthur looked at the folder that held Madden's commission. His face revealed surprise and curiosity but no trace of guilt. "What's it all about?"

"Scholarships you applied for last year."

Arthur gave him a bewildered stare and then laughed a little nervously. "I don't know why it matters to the United States Post Office but if it does, I only applied for two. A Meeker scholarship I didn't get and a National Merit scholarship which I did get and which is paying my way here."

"Well," said Madden with deep satisfaction. This was an honest kid, an innocent bystander in the Johnston fraud. He smiled at him and said, "Arthur, you're the pot of gold at the end of the rainbow and I want about an hour or so of your time. If it means one of your assignments isn't prepared for tomorrow's class I'll write an excuse to your professor myself."

Arthur grinned. "I guess I can manage without that."

"Before we start to talk I'd better check in at a motel," Madden said. "I haven't had dinner yet, either. Have you eaten?"

"Yeah, I finished just before you came." Arthur regarded him with lively interest. "Shall I keep you company while you eat or get some studying done now and meet you later?"

Madden preferred not to let him out of his sight. "You might as well come along now," he said. "I'll just check in at that motel down the road and then you can tell me the best place to have dinner and we can talk while I eat."

Twenty minutes later, seated opposite each other in a restaurant with bottles of beer in front of them, Madden ordered his dinner and settled himself to hear what Arthur Williams had to say.

"Let's start with your application for a Meeker scholarship," he suggested. "When did you send it in?"

"I talked it over with my guidance counselor in September right at the beginning of my senior year in high school. He had a folder that gave information on it and I sent for an application. I filled it in and mailed it back around the end of October. A little later, I took the exam for a National Merit scholarship. . . ."

Arthur hesitated and looked earnestly at the postal inspector. "I guess you know you have to be an orphan to be eligible for a Meeker scholarship?"

Madden nodded and he went on, "Well, both my parents are dead. I was a state ward living in a foster home. I wanted to go to college and I had to have a scholarship. A Meeker scholarship seemed just right for me. My guidance counselor was sure I qualified for one in every way.

"Two or three weeks after I sent in my application I got a letter acknowledging it and saying it would be given consideration. Then, about the first week of January I had another letter from the administrator. His name—what the heck was it now——"

"Thayer," Madden supplied.

"Yes, that was it. He wrote that he'd be in Cleveland to see me the following week and that he also wanted to talk to my high-school principal and my guidance counselor and the minister of my church and my foster parents and so on. He came the next week and had a couple of interviews with me and saw all my references. . . ."

Arthur's voice slowed. A frown appeared on his artless young face. "By the time he left Cleveland I'd have sworn I had it made from the encouragement he gave me on how far up I stood on the list and all that. Then, about the middle of March, I got another letter from him turning me down cold.

He said he was sorry but the board of trustees had rejected my application. He tried to dress it up, of course, with a lot of nice words about my qualifications being high enough for me to get some other scholarship and so forth."

Arthur was silent for a moment. Then his frown vanished. "Well, I got another one so it was all right. But when that letter first came I thought I'd had it."

"Did you ever hear from him again or write to him yourself?"

"No." Arthur paused for a swallow of beer. "There was nothing for either of us to write about. You apply for a scholarship and if you get turned down, that's it."

Not in this case, Madden thought, applying himself to his shrimp cocktail. It was only the beginning of the fraud.

A question occupied the inspector's mind as he finished the shrimp and started on vichyssoise. Why had Mrs. Meeker turned down Arthur Williams's application when she had been led to believe that he was her old friend's grandson?

He asked, "Did you send a picture of yourself with your application for a Meeker scholarship?"

"No, they didn't ask for one."

"Were you ever asked?"

"No. I never sent one."

A substitution of pictures hadn't been made.

"Were you born in Cleveland?" Madden asked next.

Arthur looked embarrassed. He said on a defensive note, "It's a heck of a thing, but I don't know my exact date of birth or where I was born. My father died when I was six months old and my mother got a job and boarded me with some people. I was only four when she was killed by a car. We were living in Cleveland but we had no relatives there or anyone who seemed to know much about us. The state had to take me over and never did find out where my people came from." He spoke rapidly without a pause as if reciting something he had learned by heart long ago.

Madden regretted probing so sensitive a spot. The boy was probably illegitimate. His unknown background had played into Thayer's hands.

Madden moved to a less personal line of inquiry. He asked, "In anything you said or wrote to Thayer did you ever suggest that if you didn't get a Meeker scholarship you might go off somewhere to make your own way in the world?"

Arthur looked startled. "Of course not. Ever since I entered high school I've been aiming for an engineering degree."

The search for Arthur Williams was a total fraud without even the flimsiest basis of fact to rest upon.

But why hadn't Mrs. Meeker accepted Arthur's application?

This question nagged at Madden as he cut into a thick slice of roast beef.

They were ordering dessert before it came to him that he had it all in the wrong sequence. Thayer hadn't conceived of the fraud when he interviewed Arthur in January 1959. At the time Arthur was no more to him than a promising applicant to be given encouragement. His concept of the fraud had a later date.

Preoccupied, letting Arthur do most of the talking, Madden worked out the way it had gone, with Thayer's telling Mrs. Meeker about seeing Arthur Williams and her saying something to the effect that she would be favorably inclined toward anyone with his name and bringing out her picture.

Then and there, perhaps, or very soon thereafter, the idea for the fraud was born and it was elaborated without a moment being lost. By the end of January, Thayer had established himself with Miss Lazinski as Henry Johnston and arranged for a telephone listing in the new directory.

Details that built up his Johnston identity, driver's license,

New York mailing address, bank account, printed stationery, and all the rest had received careful attention.

He was a coldhearted man, Joan Sheldon said. Mrs. Meeker had never warmed to him. It was quite possible that Thayer had hoped that she would in the early days of their association; had regarded her, a rich old woman, virtually alone in the world, as easy pickings. But she hadn't been. She hadn't warmed to him. A small bequest in her will, trifling out of millions, was all he'd had to anticipate from her.

He was calculating as well as coldhearted. He hadn't snatched at opportunity, he had created it himself. Perhaps he had waited years to create it, building up, in the meantime, his standing as an able, honest administrator, a man in whom Mrs. Meeker could place complete trust however little she liked him as a person. Then he had made and carried out his plan to defraud her. It had led him on to murder.

This was the framework of the case. There was much that had to be fitted into it.

Madden drank his coffee. Arthur had his undivided attention again. He asked, "Do you remember what you did with the letter of rejection Thayer sent you?"

Arthur looked puzzled. "I must have thrown it out. No, come to think of it, I didn't. It's home in a bureau drawer with some other stuff on scholarships." He shook his head ruefully. "Don't know why I kept it. It's certainly not anything I want to frame and hang on the wall."

"Would you let me have it?"

"I guess so." Arthur eyed him questioningly. "Inspector, what's this all about, anyway?"

"It's a fraud case, Arthur, originating in Medfield, Connecticut, where Mrs. Meeker, who established the scholarship fund, lived. I don't think I'd better tell you about it just yet. If it becomes a court case, you might be a government witness."

"Oh." Arthur's tone was subdued, but he looked pleasantly excited at the prospect.

Madden continued, "I noticed there was a phone booth near the cashier's desk. Will you call your foster parents in Cleveland, Arthur? I'll pay for the call. I'd like you to tell them about Thayer's letter and ask them to air-mail it to me right away."

"Okay."

"Fine. Here's the address it's to be mailed to." Madden gave him his card and a ten-dollar bill to get changed at the cashier's desk.

Arthur went away to make the call. He was gone for several minutes. When he came back he smiled at Madden with satisfaction as he handed him his change and sat down. He said, "I talked to Aunt Hilda—that's what I call my foster mother—and she looked in my bureau drawer and found the letter. She'll mail it to you first thing tomorrow morning." He grinned. "She was scared for a minute that I was in some kind of trouble."

"I hope you told her you were being a public-spirited citizen doing your government a favor," Madden said.

"Well, I didn't put it that way. I didn't know what it was supposed to be."

Madden laughed. "You can take my word for it that it's a good cause, Arthur."

They were ready to leave. Madden paid the check and drove back to the college. Outside Arthur's dormitory he thanked him and said good-by, explaining that he would return to Dunston in the morning.

He sat in his car and watched Arthur Williams go into the building. He was in no hurry to tell him, a nice, likable boy, that through the name he bore he had triggered fraud and murder.

Chapter Seventeen

MADDEN had spent most of the past two days at the wheel of his car and felt the effects of it the next morning. He took his time on the drive back to Dunston, not getting there until the early evening. While he was on the road he thought over what Arthur Williams had told him, accepting or rejecting the inferences he drew from it until he arrived at what seemed to him a fairly accurate reconstruction of the whole fraud.

It was Friday. Tad had gone home to Delaware for the weekend.

Madden found Thayer's letter to Arthur Williams, airmailed from Cleveland, on his desk Monday morning. He read Thayer's smoothly worded expressions of regret that Arthur's application had not been approved, let Tad read it, and passed it on to the clerk with instructions to get a photostatic copy of it right off to the Bureau for a comparison of Thayer's signature with Johnston's right-hand Amarillo signature and ask for a TWX reply. Then he sat down with Tad to tell him what he had learned from Arthur Williams and the conclusions he had drawn from it.

"I can't believe Mrs. Meeker turned him down for a scholarship," he said. "Not with all she was ready to do later on to find him. We know that Thayer set up the fraud in January; but with Mrs. Meeker taking a personal interest in Arthur, Thayer, whether it was part of his plan or not, had to let

Arthur's application come before the board and be approved in March.

"After he wrote Arthur that his application had been rejected, I don't think he made his next real move until June. He certainly wouldn't want to show what was supposed to be Arthur's picture to Mrs. Meeker too early in the game. It would make a more plausible story that a good student like Arthur would wait to graduate from high school before he left Cleveland."

Madden continued, "Pictures weren't sent with applications so he'd have to tell Mrs. Meeker that he'd noticed how much Arthur resembled the one she had of her old friend and that he'd asked Arthur for his picture to let her see the resemblance for herself."

Madden spoke slowly, looking for flaws in his theory as he put it into words. "If I'd been in Thayer's place, I'd have let her make up her own mind that this must be her Arthur's grandson. She was so opinionated, I might even oppose the idea at first to make her twice as sure she was right. Immediately, she'd want more information on Arthur's background. It's a fair assumption that Thayer pretended to write for it or to go out there himself to get it.

"However he worked it, faked letter or phone call or trip, he came back to Mrs. Meeker with the story that Arthur had turned down the scholarship and gone off to Texas to make his own way in the world. Thayer had two strings to his bow there. Texas, where her Arthur had spent most of his life, would clinch her belief that this was his grandson; and with Ulysses S. Meeker an orphan who had made his own way it created a parallel that was bound to appeal enormously to Mrs. Meeker."

"But suppose she'd insisted on getting in touch with Arthur's foster parents in Cleveland," Tad inserted. "The whole thing would have fallen apart right then and there."

"Oh, you can be sure Thayer took care of that," Madden replied. "He pretended he went out there to see them or phoned them or composed a letter they were supposed to have written professing no knowledge of where Arthur had gone. He could make them cruel foster parents. He could say they'd become estranged from Arthur or whatever he thought would best guarantee Mrs. Meeker's not seeking their help."

After a pause Madden added, "That's about it, I think. In her senility she was hooked and ready to hire a private detective and pay him enormous fees to find Arthur Williams."

"How do you suppose Thayer worked in the insurance friend who recommended Johnston to her?"

Madden shrugged. "He must have had some angle on it as phony as everything else in the setup."

"Including whatever approach he used to get the extra fifty thousand out of her," Tad supplemented.

"Yes, including that." The inspector looked at his watch. It was nearly eleven o'clock by now. Close to nine, he thought, Mountain time in Colorado.

"I'm not going to wait for a letter from Dr. Greer," he informed Tad. "I want to hear what he has to say about that board meeting last year."

He got out Dr. Greer's Boulder, Colorado, address and put in a person-to-person call to him.

Dr. Greer was soon reached. He came on the phone and when Madden introduced himself said, "Oh yes, Inspector. Your letter came Saturday. I wrote to you last night and put it in the mail to go out this morning. I remember the Williams boy. It was an unusual situation. We approved his application for a full, four-year scholarship and had a very nice letter of thanks from him. Then, a couple of months later, he turned it down flat and went off somewhere on his own. These young people nowadays. So restless. Half of them don't know what they want. It's the times, I suppose."

Dr. Greer continued, "I follow the scholarships closely— my field was education—and keep a private record on the applicants who are approved. The notes I made on Williams are still in my file at home."

Unlike Mr. Weltner, his fellow trustee, Dr. Greer spoke without vagueness and in a businesslike tone that revealed no tremor of age. He did not suggest that Thayer would have all this information available. He had the good sense to assume that Madden had his own reasons for writing and then phoning him in Colorado.

The inspector, giving him full credit for this, asked, "Is there any way, with you in Colorado, Doctor, that I could get to see your notes on Williams?"

"Why, yes, I think you could. Mrs. Greer left a key with Sarah Black, our cleaning woman, who goes in to keep things dusted and water the plants and so forth."

Dr. Greer supplied the cleaning woman's address and went on to tell Madden that he kept the scholarship records in his study and exactly where they were to be found.

"I'm going out to Medfield now," Madden said. "Will you be available if Sarah Black objects to letting me in your house and I have her call you for permission?"

"Yes, but she won't object. She's a very easygoing woman. Probably offer you the key to go yourself."

Madden laughed. "I won't have that. There's just one thing more, Doctor. Would you mind if I borrowed your notes on Williams?"

"I don't see why you shouldn't. There's really no reason for me to keep them at all since he didn't accept his scholarship."

Dr. Greer exercised tact and restraint to the very end. He

asked no questions as Madden thanked him and said good-by.

Before he left the building Madden went down the hall to the United States district attorney's office and arranged to see one of his assistants later in the day to talk over the evidence of fraud he was accumulating against Thayer. Then he set out with Tad for Sarah Black's in Medfield.

Just as Dr. Greer had predicted, she raised no objections to giving them access to his house although she didn't offer them the key as he had thought she might, but went with them and hovered in the study doorway while Madden looked through the scholarship records and took out the notes on Arthur Williams.

Under the date of March 18, 1959, Arthur's full name and address, high-school record, college of choice, and proposed course of study had been listed by Dr. Greer. Then he had written: "Thayer speaks highly of, considers exceptionally promising. Must follow progress closely." Beneath this came the final notation: "June 19, 1959: Mrs. M. just called. Said Wms. has refused scholarship in letter to Thayer. Going to Texas to look for job. Don't know why it upset Mrs. M. so much. Flew into a temper when I mentioned making a second choice for vacant scholarship."

Madden had Sarah Black initial the notes before he took them away with him. When they had dropped her off at her house Tad commented, "Thayer could have turned out a book in the time he spent writing all his fancy letters."

"I know," Madden said. "The amount of time and effort people put into fraudulent schemes would make them an honest fortune." He added, heading his car toward the center of town, "We'd better stop and see the chief. We're out of touch with him."

They drove to police headquarters and saw Pauling. When

Madden had brought him up to date on his own activities, he asked Pauling how he was making out himself.

The police chief said that he still had his man in Philadelphia pursuing suburban car rentals but might as well bring him back, considering his total lack of success. The man he had sent to Red Bank had returned Saturday and reported that Thayer had a good reputation in his home town. The only knowledge the Red Bank police had of him was that fourteen or fifteen years ago he had been involved in a car accident in Trenton, a head-on collision with another car whose driver had been killed. No blame had been attached to Thayer, however. He had been seriously injured himself and the driver of the other car was held wholly responsible for the accident. Since it had occurred in Trenton, the Red Bank police had no file on it. For the rest, Thayer had led an uneventful, law-abiding life in Red Bank from childhood on.

"The accident hardly seems worth following up," Pauling said in conclusion.

"I guess not." Madden hesitated. "I wonder what kind of injuries, though."

"What kind . . . ? Oh, the alibi of head injuries, you mean, if he stands trial."

"Yes." Madden smiled. "But let's be optimistic and say when, not if."

"You going to bring him in for questioning?" Pauling inquired. "You've got plenty of evidence against him on the fraud. Hell, I wish I had half of it on the murder."

Madden said, "I want to be sure I can make it stick before I bring him in. I'll talk it over with an assistant U.S. attorney as soon as I get back to Dunston. Thayer will keep. At least I hope he will."

"We're keeping an eye on him all we can. If he makes a

move to leave town we'll bring him in." Pauling added with the bitterness of frustration, "Idleness or breach of the peace when he should be charged with murder."

"We'll have to keep trying." Madden had no better answer to give. As he stood up to go he said that he would be back tomorrow. He said next, "If I don't bring him in I'll put some pressure on him and see what comes of it."

"At his apartment?"

"I think so. And on my own, if you don't mind. We don't want him to claim duress later by saying we were all on his neck at once. I'll drop by after I've seen him."

They left it like that. Madden and Tad went back to Dunston and saw the assistant United States attorney. Madden went over the evidence he had accumulated with him.

"Strong circumstantial evidence," he commented. "Very strong."

He was a youngish man. He leaned back in his chair, frowned at the ceiling, took off his glasses, tapped the stems against the bridge of his nose, and put them on again. He said at last, "I wish we had a little more concrete evidence of fraud, though. If we can't get it—well, we'll give it to the grand jury and if they indict, take it to court as it stands."

This was about the legal opinion he'd expected, Madden told Tad when they left the assistant United States attorney.

It was almost five o'clock. They were ready to call it a day. It started to rain. Madden decided to cook his own dinner at home.

Chapter Eighteen

THE morning brought a speedy TWX reply to Madden's latest inquiry from the Bureau in Washington. It said that common authorship of Thayer's signature on Arthur Williams's letter and Johnston's Amarillo signature was definitely indicated.

"Nothing more to wait for," Madden said to Tad. "We'd better find out first, though, if Thayer's home."

He phoned Pauling, who said that to the best of his knowledge Thayer hadn't left his apartment this morning.

The postal inspector was silent during the drive to Medfield, thinking about what might develop from his interview with Thayer. When they were almost at the apartment house, he said, "After we're there a few minutes, Tad, ask to use the bathroom. If you can get into the bedroom too, fine. Take a good look around. Bottle of hair dye or rinse in the medicine cabinet, flashy clothes, eyeglasses, papers, anything. He's probably got rid of it all but it won't hurt to take a look."

They parked near the apartment building. A police cruiser manned by two officers came up behind their car and stopped. One of the officers got out and walked over to them. Pauling, he said, had notified him of their impending arrival and wanted them to know that a foot patrolman had been moved over from the nearby business district to walk a beat in the neighborhood. He would be around if they wanted him for anything; also, the cruiser, supplementing his watch, kept an eye on Thayer's car and would be back and forth.

Madden thanked the officer and said that he expected to be with Thayer for the next hour or more.

The cruiser drove away. Far down the street a blue-uniformed figure turned the corner toward them. The cruiser stopped beside it.

"It's a surveillance full of holes, if you ask me," Tad remarked as they approached the apartment building.

"Probably the best Pauling can do on a continuing basis with no arrest in sight," Madden said. "He doesn't have too big a force, and he's had a lot of his men tied up on the murder."

They rode up in the self-service elevator to Thayer's apartment on the fourth floor. He came to the door, greeted them with his customary self-possession, and took them into his office.

When they were seated he waited for Madden to explain his visit. It was a habit of his, Madden had noticed. Silences didn't disconcert him. He waited with every show of calmness.

The inspector set out to put a dent in it. "I went to see Arthur Williams the other day," he said. "You may be interested to know that he got another scholarship, Mr. Thayer. He's at Clarkson."

"Arthur Williams?" A note of surprise from Thayer. "The one Mrs. Meeker——"

"Yes, that one; the one you turned down for a Meeker scholarship."

"I turned him down?" Thayer looked rueful. "Lord, I'm slipping. I don't even recall his name."

"Let me refresh your memory. You interviewed him, his high school principal and all his other references a year ago last January in Cleveland."

"Well, I interview hundreds of boys, year in, year out. Unless they're awarded Meeker scholarships—Cleveland, you said?" Thayer wasn't giving an inch. The puzzled look on his colorless, unremarkable face might almost have been genuine.

Madden, conscious of Tad beside him prepared to learn from his handling of the interrogation, said sharply, "Mr. Thayer, Williams was accepted by the board on March 18, 1959, and then rejected by you as part of your scheme to defraud Mrs. Meeker. You've destroyed the file on him, of course, and all the phony papers and letters you fixed up. How did you doctor up the minutes of the meeting? May I see them?"

"Certainly. They are not doctored up." Thayer got to his feet and went to a filing cabinet. He took out a sheaf of papers stapled together and handed them to the postal inspector.

He read them. The meeting had been held in the afternoon at Mrs. Meeker's. Present were Mrs. Meeker and Dr. Greer; absent, Mr. Weltner. The meeting had been called to order at 3:00 P.M. Mrs. Meeker, chairman, had presided. The only item on the agenda was the selection of scholarship recipients for the coming year. Brian Thayer, administrator, had presented a list of applicants for the board's consideration. Arthur Williams's name was not on it; it was not on the list of those who were awarded scholarships. There were no erasures. Thayer had made a new copy of the minutes.

Madden returned them to him and asked, "Who's the secretary?"

"The girl who works part-time for me."

Madden asked for her name and address and wrote them down. He would see her later, although he knew that nothing was less likely than that she would remember the names of last year's scholarship winners.

Thayer seemed to have the same thought. His tone was confident as he gave the girl's name and address. He added,

"I hope you're satisfied, Inspector, that Williams, whoever he is, was not approved or even considered at the board meeting. I'll take your word for it that he applied for a Meeker scholarship although I don't have the least recollection of him myself."

"What became of his application? You said you'd kept all of them so far, approved or rejected."

Thayer shrugged off the question. "I didn't say that none of the rejects had ever been inadvertently destroyed. My secretary—you know what part-time help is."

Tad stood up. "May I use your bathroom, Mr. Thayer?"

"Certainly. It's down the hall, the door on the right next to the bedroom."

"Thank you." Tad left the room. The bedroom as well as the bathroom would be accessible to him.

Madden got to his feet, walked across the room, and turned back to Thayer. He said, "I talked with Dr. Greer in Colorado yesterday. Did you know he kept his own records on scholarship recipients?"

Thayer's glance flickered away. He was shaken at last. He hadn't known. Dr. Greer was a man who kept his own counsel.

Madden continued, "He arranged for me to get hold of his notes on Arthur Williams. Let me read them to you." He reached into his pocket, brought them out, and read them aloud.

The light from the window picked out a beading of sweat on Thayer's forehead. The veiled look of his eyes indicated that his mind was very busy.

Madden said next, "The board awarded a scholarship to Williams on March 18. I have a copy here of a letter you wrote to him on March 20 telling him his application had been turned down. Shall I read it to you?"

Thayer shook his head. He took out a handkerchief and

meticulously wiped his face with it. He sighed and said, "I keep trying to cover up Mrs. Meeker's foibles but I can see it is no use."

He sat down. Madden sat down opposite him, waiting to hear what fabrication he would offer.

He began, "Mrs. Meeker called me up the day after the board meeting and said she'd changed her mind about Williams. Write him a letter that his application was rejected, destroy it and forget I ever heard of him. I carried out these instructions and crossed Williams's name off the approved list before the minutes were typed. She gave no reason for her action then or later when she decided she wanted him found. She said she would tell Dr. Greer about it herself but it seems from his notes that she waited until June to do it. . . ."

Thayer's face took on a perplexed expression. "I don't understand it. Or why she told him then that Williams had turned down the scholarship instead of admitting that she had refused to let him have it. It was her money, of course, but even so——" He came to a full halt. Then he said, "I felt it was her age that led to her eccentricities. She'd lost more ground than most people realized these last couple of years. I was fully aware of the change in her, though. I had a lot to cope with that I kept to myself."

He went on talking about Mrs. Meeker's mental lapses. Madden listened in cold silence until Thayer's voice lost impetus and sweat beaded his forehead again. He wiped it off. He said, "I know you don't like it that I told you Arthur Williams had never applied for a scholarship, but——"

"But you respected Mrs. Meeker's eccentricities," Madden filled in for him. "With the safe-deposit box it was her wishes you respected. Really, Thayer, are you going to have the effrontery to get up on the witness stand and tell these tales out loud to a jury and United States attorney?"

"I won't have to. If I did, I'd be telling the truth."

"The truth? Come now, Thayer, you wouldn't know it if you met it."

Thayer made no reply. His face kept its composure. Only his eyes, their glance wandering around the room, betrayed his uneasiness.

In a deliberate tone Madden proceeded to bring up other points calculated to reveal how much knowledge he had of the fraud to Thayer.

Whatever he mentioned, Thayer denied. Mrs. Meeker had never shown him her picture of Arthur Williams. He knew nothing of photography or composite pictures. He knew nothing of handwriting, either. If post-office experts found similarities between his signature and Johnston's, well, lots of people had similar handwriting, he supposed.

This was Thayer's attitude toward all of the inspector's statements and questions on the workings of the fraud. But now his hands as well as his eyes betrayed his uneasiness. They would clinch on the arms of his chair until the knuckles were white. He would loosen them, put them in his lap, but they would soon find their way back to the chair arms and clinch tight again.

The murder of Mrs. Meeker hung unmentioned in the air between them.

Tad came back into the room. His headshake told Madden that his search for some piece of incriminating evidence had been fruitless.

Madden tried to increase the pressure. He said, "I'd like further specimens of your handwriting, Mr. Thayer. You tell me you're an innocent man so you certainly have nothing to fear from giving them to me."

A guarded look from Thayer. Then he said, "No, I have nothing to fear," and stood up and went to his desk.

"You want my signature again, I presume?" He seated himself and reached for a sheet of paper.

"Yes. Left- and right-hand. A Johnston signature, too, left- and right-hand." Madden moved to the desk and watched him write "Brian Thayer" at the top of the sheet with his right hand and shift the pen to his left. As he watched, he caught the significance he had missed once before in the way Thayer handled the pen. He had started to bring it up and around on the paper, checked himself, and scrawled his signature holding the pen the same way he had held it in his right hand. He didn't let it happen again with the Johnston signature; he simply transferred the pen from his right hand to his left. Then he blotted the signatures and handed the paper across the desk to Madden.

"Thank you." Madden folded it, put it in his pocket, and said next, "You know, I noticed when you did this for me at Mrs. Meeker's that you had a little more trouble with left-hand signatures than the others. Now I know why."

"Do you?"

"People who are naturally left-handed bring the pen up and around on the paper to write as you started to do. When right-handed people use the left hand they hold the pen just as they would with their right and make a botch of it. I think you were born with an ambidextrous tendency. It may have been latent until you suffered an injury to your right arm. Didn't it get broken, possibly a very bad break, in your auto accident in Trenton years ago?"

In shocked silence Thayer looked at him.

Madden continued, "You were seriously injured. Let's say you lost the use of your right arm for several months. Did your ambidextrous trait come out when you started learning to write with your left hand or were you taught by a left-handed person?"

Thayer said nothing.

Madden continued in the same level tone, "Hospital records in Trenton will tell us what your injuries were. Life is
full of records, Thayer. We never get away from them from
the day our birth record goes on file. Now, if you'll write your
name again with your left hand using the up-and-around
method, I don't doubt that our laboratory in Washington will
find it practically identical to the Johnston signatures we've
picked up here and there."

Thayer could take no more. He sprang to his feet. "Get out
of here," he said through his teeth. "I've put up with enough
from you. Get out!"

Hands in his pockets, the inspector looked at him. Thayer
was beside himself with fear and rage. Goaded into the wrong
move at last?

Madden hoped so. He turned to Tad, who was on his feet
ready for whatever action seemed indicated, and said, "Mr.
Thayer is tired of our company, Tad. Shall we go?"

Tad shot him an astonished glance, recovered himself, and
replied, "If you say so, Inspector."

They made their departure with Thayer watching them
from the door of his office.

"I thought you had him on the run," Tad burst out as soon
as the apartment door was shut behind them. "And then——"

"That's exactly what I want," Madden said. "He won't run
without Mrs. Meeker's money. He's got it put away somewhere."

They went along the hall to the elevator and had it to themselves on the way down. Madden said, "You heard a legal
opinion yesterday, Tad, on the gaps in our evidence. If we
got a conviction on it, Thayer would still be getting away
with Mrs. Meeker's murder. A helpless old woman smothered
with a pillow. It's the murder I want to see him charged with."

They left the elevator and went out of the building. Thayer's front windows overlooked the street. He would be watching to see what they would do. Madden took care not to glance up. His gaze settled on a green Ford convertible parked in front of the apartment house. It was Thayer's. He had seen it at Mrs. Meeker's. He said, "He'll never go without the money."

"How do we stay close to him?" Tad inquired. "He'll be on his toes every minute to see if he's being followed. He'll probably come out of the building with a spyglass in his hand."

"Spyglass," Madden said. "What are we issued binoculars for? I haven't got mine with me. How about the drugstore around the corner? We don't need good ones. Any pair will do."

The patrolman assigned to the neighborhood was nowhere in sight.

They got into the car. If Thayer were watching from a window, he would see them drive away.

Madden stopped in front of the drugstore. While Tad was inside he walked back to the corner to keep an eye on Thayer's car. It still stood at the curb two blocks away. If Thayer meant to run, he must be rushing around his apartment right now getting ready for it.

Tad returned with the binoculars. Madden took them from him and said, "I'd like you to keep an eye on Thayer's car while I go up around the next street. Give me two or three minutes and then go back to the drugstore and call Pauling. Tell him what's developed and ask him if he doesn't think roads out of Medfield should be covered. He needn't close in on the apartment, though. Tell him I'm covering it. When you come back to the car go around the next block yourself so Thayer won't see you. If you run into the patrolman—he probably thinks we're still with Thayer—keep him out of sight."

Tad moved to the corner. Madden turned up the next street and turned back onto Thayer's street two blocks above the apartment house. He braked to a stop and shut off the motor. The green convertible stood where he had seen it last. He unwrapped the binoculars and adjusted them to his vision. The entrance to the apartment house loomed large through their lenses; the green convertible appeared to be only a few feet away. They would do for his purpose. He put them down on the seat and settled back to wait.

He hoped for a long enough wait to give Pauling time to act. This hope had hardly registered in his mind, however, when a man came out of the apartment building. Madden picked up the binoculars and Thayer, carrying a raincoat but without luggage, sprang into his view. He paused on the step and looked up and down the street. Cars parked closer to him than Madden's inconspicuous black Chevy were given a seemingly casual scrutiny. Then, without haste, Thayer got into his own car. He put the top down. It was a mild April afternoon, but what he had in mind, Madden thought, was a wider range of vision behind him.

He started the motor and drove away.

Madden knew that Pauling couldn't possibly have arranged for roads out of town to be covered in the few minutes since Tad had phoned him. There was no sign of Tad himself. He hadn't had nearly enough time to get back to the car on foot. It was going to be Madden's all the way.

Chapter Nineteen

HE took his time. He started the motor but let a truck go past him. Through the binoculars he saw that the green convertible remained stationary at the end of the street until the truck came close enough for Thayer to satisfy himself the driver was what he seemed. Then Thayer made a right turn that would take him past the drugstore. Starting after him, Madden could only hope that Tad was still inside or out of sight on the next street.

At the stop sign he looked to his right. No sign of Tad, no chance to pick him up, but the green convertible was parked only a block away. Thayer was still checking.

Madden turned left on the through street and drove with his gaze on the rear-view mirror until the green convertible was well behind him. Then he turned around at a gas station, waited for another car to get in front of him and headed back toward Thayer.

He drove slowly. He saw Thayer pull out from the curb apparently satisfied for the moment that no one followed him.

Depending on quick glances through the binoculars, Madden kept his distance, letting other cars get between them.

They skirted the business district and left it behind. Presently a highway sign indicated an intersection ahead. The green convertible turned right at the intersection. When Madden reached it himself he saw an arrow pointing to the Connecticut Turnpike. Thayer was heading for it, he thought, and driving faster now, apparently confident at last that he wasn't being followed.

They had taken a main road at the intersection and were on it for half an hour in fairly heavy traffic. It seemed safe to Madden to close up the gap between the two cars a little.

A sign announced a feeder road to the turnpike east. When the green convertible turned off on it Madden slowed down considerably, allowing several cars to take it ahead of him. It wound uphill a little before it sloped down to the turnpike entrance. At the crest of the rise Madden saw the green convertible pulled over to the side of the road below while Thayer checked on the cars in back of him. As Madden watched he drove out onto the turnpike and immediately picked up speed.

Following him, Madden hoped that this was the last check Thayer would make.

They traveled the turnpike for the best part of an hour, staying within the speed limit—Thayer apparently wanted no state trooper stopping him—Madden keeping a good distance behind, closing up a little at exits and toll booths but not enough to attract Thayer's attention.

They were well into eastern Connecticut when Madden, as he passed a sign that said next exit two miles, saw that far ahead of him Thayer had started to slow down, and reduced his own speed. When Thayer's brake lights and direction signal for a right turn flashed on, Madden began to draw up on him, not knowing where he was headed when he left the turnpike.

Thayer's car turned off at the exit and vanished around a curve with the postal inspector closer behind than he had been the whole time, taking the chance that Thayer felt confident enough now not to stop for another check on cars in back of him.

Madden came around the curve himself to a blacktop secondary road in time to see the green convertible disappearing from sight on his left. A sign pointing that way read Bridgeville, four miles. It was an eastern Connecticut town not far from the shore line. If the inspector had ever been there, he had no memory of it.

Those four miles on a winding road were the most difficult of all, he discovered. Country roads led off it on either side, any one of which Thayer might take without his knowledge, since he didn't dare try to keep the convertible in sight and had only occasional glimpses of it in the distance.

He counted on a bank, though, as Thayer's destination and kept reminding himself of this each time he passed a side road. None would lead to a bank. Bridgeville was Thayer's likeliest objective.

The road straightened out within the town limits and became a street with sidewalks and houses and a thirty-mile speed limit that Thayer observed meticulously as he took a right turn toward the center. Madden stayed so far behind he had to resort to the binoculars to keep track of him at all.

Bridgeville was a pretty little town. The center consisted of scattered stores set down among houses on the tree-shaded main street. Thayer made a left turn off it and was lost to view. Madden thought that it was a side street he had taken and had to brake to a quick stop when Thayer came walking around the side of a red brick building, climbed the front steps, and went inside.

The inspector drew abreast of it and with immense satisfaction saw "Bridgeville Savings Bank" lettered in the stone lintel above the entrance. It was a small bank with shrubbery and a green lawn spangled with dandelion blossoms in front of it. Thayer's car was in the parking lot beside the building.

Madden left his car across the street. He kept out of the line of vision the plate-glass door offered to those inside as he moved toward it. He had his gun on him. Mostly it was a nuisance, but a new directive from Washington made it mandatory that inspectors go armed at all times. This once he was glad that he had his gun and didn't have to go into a country bank empty-handed to deal with a murderer on the run.

He took a quick look through the door. A woman at one of the teller stations was the only visible customer. Thayer was somewhere out of sight, probably in the safe-deposit vault.

The inspector opened the door and went in. On his right were three teller stations with the woman customer at one of them. On his left two bank officials sat inside an enclosure. The safe-deposit vault was in the rear with a metal gate opening into the space in front of it. The custodian stood inside the gate.

It might take more time than he could afford, Madden thought, to explain himself to the officials. He walked quietly to the rear. His gun was in a shoulder holster, his right hand near it on the lapel of his unbuttoned jacket. In his left he held his identification folder.

The custodian watched him approach. Madden made a shushing sound to impress the need for silence, held out his folder, and asked under his breath, "Is there a man back here opening his box?"

The startled custodian ruined it all. He looked at the folder and stammered much louder than was necessary, "Why, yes —yes, Inspector."

Thayer flashed out of a cubicle around the corner. His gun covered Madden a split second before he could draw his own. The custodian had his back turned to him. When he spun around it was far too late to make any move.

A high wood partition hid Thayer from the rest of the bank personnel. He said in a low voice to the custodian, "Open the gate and let him in." And to Madden, "Don't make a sound. I'll shoot my way out of here if I have to."

With shaking fingers the custodian pressed the button that opened the gate. Madden stepped through it and it clanged shut behind him.

"Back this way," Thayer said. Madden and the custodian moved back into a corridor off which the cubicles opened. Now they were all completely out of sight of the bank personnel.

"Stand far apart, get your hands up and turn your faces to the wall," Thayer said.

They did as they were told. Thayer came toward them warily, his gun at their backs as he relieved them of theirs.

His breathing was quick and shallow, loud in the backwater of quiet that surrounded them.

A moment of silence followed while he thought out his next move. Then he said, "Guard, you're my hostage until I get out of here. You'll walk with me to the door. Inspector, stay where you are. One move, one sound out of you and I shoot the guard and anyone else who gets in my way. Is that clear?"

"Yes," Madden said.

The front door of the bank opened and closed on a cheerful good-by from the woman customer. She had left. That made one person less to get in the way of a bullet. If there were one.

Thayer picked up a brief case and withdrew with the custodian. When Madden heard the gate shut behind them, he came out of the corridor and saw Thayer and the custodian walking side by side to the door. He couldn't see the tellers from where he stood but the two officials were still at their desks inside the enclosure.

He could only wait, powerless to make a move, aware of the deadly intent behind Thayer's threats. He would shoot the custodian, anyone who tried to stop him if Madden raised the alarm. He had nothing to lose. He was already a murderer.

Madden advanced to the gate. Now he could look outside through the glass door. A man and woman were coming up the walk to the bank. The tellers were all away from their stations at their desks. No one but Madden saw Thayer reverse his gun and slash the custodian with vicious force on the back of the head. He made a sound between a grunt and a moan and dropped to the floor. Thayer rushed past him out of the bank, barely avoiding a collision on the steps with the pair who were on their way into it.

The staff awakened to trouble at last. One officer rushed out of the enclosure to the custodian, the other turned toward Madden, who got the gate open and called out, "Ring your alarm!"

The officer who knelt beside the custodian echoed, "Ring it!" A woman teller pressed the holdup-alarm button at her station.

The pair coming into the bank stopped short on the threshold in amazement.

Madden said, "I'm Postal Inspector Madden," to the other officer, and thrust his identification folder at him. He glanced at it and began to sputter questions.

Madden explained hurriedly that the bank hadn't been robbed, that this was a fraud and murder case. He reeled off the make, color, and license number of Thayer's car to be passed on to the police and asked to borrow a gun. The moment he had one in his hands he ran to the door.

Now he had a piece of the luck that had deserted him entirely inside the bank. A teen-age boy talking to a girl out in front had noticed Thayer's car and was able to tell the inspector that it had turned right coming out of the parking lot.

Madden flung a thank you at him over his shoulder, followed by the afterthought that the boy should tell this to the police when they arrived. He ran across the street to his car, made a U-turn that drew a sharp blast of the horn from an approaching driver, and started in pursuit of Thayer. He was heading for the turnpike, Madden thought.

Bridgeville, he thought next, was a small town. He didn't know how much of a police force it had, how close the nearest state police barracks was, or how fast, with their help, a road block could be set up. He had to conclude that for the present, at least, he was still on his own.

He drove faster than was altogether safe through Bridgeville's scattered business center. The gun the bank had supplied, a Colt .38, lay on the seat beside him.

He had left the town behind and was well on his way back to the turnpike when he saw in the distance a big trailer truck crawling up a long winding hill and behind it a green car. He looked through the binoculars and gave a sigh of relief. The car trapped behind the trailer truck was Thayer's. Madden shot ahead, gaining ground rapidly.

Thayer spotted him in the rear-view mirror. With total disregard for danger he swung out to pass the truck on a curve but had to pull back to avoid a head-on collision with an oncoming car. The truck and Thayer's car went around the curve out of sight. The oncoming car passed Madden before he went around the curve himself and came out on a straight stretch that brought him to the top of the hill. The truck was already descending it but Thayer's car had vanished.

It took Madden a split second to recall a glimpse of a side road, one of those he had worried about on his way to Bridgeville—good God, it was only half an hour ago—just this side of the curve. Thayer had turned off on it.

Madden braked to a screeching stop, put his car in reverse, and backed down the hill to the side road.

He found it narrow and bumpy and indifferently paved. A farmhouse stood alongside it a few hundred feet in from the highway, but there was no one in the yard to confirm his belief that this was the road Thayer had taken. There was no sign of him at all until Madden came to a fork in the road.

Which way? Last night's rain furnished the answer. Thayer, taking the left fork, had driven through a puddle and left wet tire marks on the cracked asphalt surface.

Madden took the left fork. He passed a dilapidated farmhouse with boarded-up windows.

The road, full of potholes, became deplorable. He had to slow down. But so did Thayer.

He passed the ruins of a shack. Then there were only woods and underbrush. Thayer's luck had been out when he chose the left fork. This unused road led nowhere and would soon peter out entirely, Madden thought. If he hadn't missed a dead-end sign along it, then the sign had been removed or fallen apart.

He came to an old logging road. Flattened weeds and grass at the entrance caught his eye. He drove past it and went on around the next bend before he stopped, shut off the motor, and got out, the gun in his hand. Swiftly and silently he made his way back to the logging road. Underbrush opposite it afforded cover. He eased himself down behind it and waited, taut and still. It wouldn't be for long, he thought. Thayer must be straining the limits of his caution, frantic to get back to the other fork in the road, the highway, any road that would let him out of the trap he found himself in.

Even as this thought went through the inspector's mind he heard a car start up on the logging road.

It was headed out when it came into view from among the trees. Thayer had backed it in. He kept both hands on the wheel to steer it on the rutted track. When he reached the edge of the road he came to an almost complete stop and looked both ways for Madden. One of his hands dropped down out of sight—to close on the butt of his gun or Madden's or the custodian's. He was a murderer in flight with three guns to choose from.

Madden fired and shot a hole through the radiator. Steam hissed and water spurted out of the grille. He flattened himself against the ground while four shots whipped over his head, one fairly close, the others wild.

The car door slammed. He raised himself enough for a quick look through the underbrush and saw Thayer dart into the woods. He called out to him to halt and raced across the road in a crouch to the shelter of the car. Thayer whirled around, sent two very wild shots in his direction, and started running again.

"Halt and drop your gun or I'll shoot!" Madden raised his gun to eye level. Thayer flung away his empty gun and kept running. Madden aimed for his middle and fired.

The bullet caught Thayer in the shoulder. He screamed, stumbled forward into a tree, and went down, his right hand clutching at his other shoulder. Blood spread rapidly over the sleeve.

Madden held his gun ready as he moved toward him. "Where are the other guns?" he asked.

"My God, are you going to let me bleed to death?" Thayer gasped. "My coat pocket . . ." He rolled over on his uninjured side and revealed a pocket sagging with the weight of the two revolvers. Madden took possession of them and removed the cartridges.

"A doctor—get a doctor quick." There was no fight, no threat left in Thayer.

Madden made a pad of a clean handkerchief to check the bleeding. It was already lessening. There was bone fracture though, he suspected, and used both their belts to make a support that held the arm firm against Thayer's body. He had to help him to his feet and all the way around the bend to his car.

The brief case he'd carried at the bank lay on the seat of his car. Madden stopped to pick it up and took it with him.

His face pale and drawn, Thayer slumped down in the seat beside the inspector as they drove to the nearest habitation, the farmhouse off the highway. He had to be helped into the house.

The telephone was a wall instrument in the kitchen. Thayer sank onto a kitchen chair provided by the flustered housewife, who was the only person home.

With one eye on him Madden phoned the Bridgeville police station.

"A doctor," Thayer said.

"They'll bring one."

While he waited for the police to arrive Madden opened the brief case. It was filled with money, packages of it in envelopes from the Bronx bank. One envelope, larger and bulkier than the others, had the name of Mrs. Meeker's Dunston bank on it. Madden counted the money it contained. It came to an even fifty thousand dollars.

The housewife's eyes popped. Thayer looked on in sullen despair.

Madden didn't count the rest. "I suppose it will be close to all that you took her for," he said without emphasis. "Killed her for."

Thayer defended himself with a sudden flash of energy. "She'd have had no mercy on me if I'd let her live to talk to you the next day. She'd have sent me to prison without a second thought. My job would be gone, my reputation, my whole future—all the plans I'd been making for it—I'd have lost everything."

"You've lost everything, anyway," Madden informed him. "And added murder to it."

Thayer said nothing. Presently, in a spiritless voice, he asked for a glass of water.

Madden felt exhausted himself. He felt as if it were a century ago that he'd had to leave Tad stranded in Medfield— and how disappointed Tad would be to have missed the climax—to take up the pursuit of Thayer. There was no sense of elation that success had crowned his efforts. Not yet, at least. An old woman asleep in her bed and a man less than half her age and twice her strength making a stealthy entrance to smother her with a pillow was not a foeman worthy of decent steel.

Madden could only look at him with tired distaste.

Car doors slammed outside. The police had arrived.

Chapter Twenty

"IF only she hadn't called Hartford at the wrong time," Thayer said. "If it hadn't been for that . . ."

He was brooding aloud. "I wasn't going to keep it up much longer. I was even thinking about the report I'd write telling her I'd run out of leads on Arthur Williams and that I was taking another case out West. After a few letters back and forth the whole thing would have gradually died out. Then I meant to start investing the money a little at a time. Good growth stocks, utilities. I had a solid program all worked out. . . ."

Madden recalled a newspaper open at stock-market reports in Thayer's office. He had brightened his curiously barren life, it seemed, with daydreams about future investments. Joan Sheldon had called him a coldhearted man; but money, at least, had warmed his heart.

"The love of money is the root of all evil." Madden dug into his memory. Timothy, wasn't it?

The loss of it had broken Thayer. The consequences of murder actually came second with him, Madden thought. Or perhaps, like many another murderer before him, he had already persuaded himself that he would somehow evade them.

Two days had passed since Thayer had been taken from the Bridgeville farmhouse to a New London hospital. Yesterday morning after considerable repair work his fractured shoulder had been set and he had been kept under sedation the rest of the day. Now he had been pronounced fit for questioning, and Madden and Tad Chandler, Pauling and a Medfield police sergeant taking notes were assembled in his hospital room.

A nurse had provided extra chairs. It looked like a deathbed scene, Madden thought sardonically; the family gathered around a dying man to hear his last words.

Thayer, however, was in no present danger of becoming a corpse. But his usual look of calm self-assurance had vanished. Propped up in bed, his upper arm in a cast, he had a quenched look, a collapsed-puppet look of final and utter defeat. In spite of the pains he had taken, the time and attention devoted to every detail, his undetectable fraud and the undetectable murder it led to had come down in ruins around his head.

This was made clear to him at the start of the hospital interview.

Two days ago, as soon as he had seen Thayer removed to the hospital under guard, Madden, shaking off fatigue, had gone back to work on the case.

The custodian hadn't been seriously injured, he learned, when he returned to the bank with the Bridgeville police chief. It was long past closing time when he got there, but the staff had been asked to wait for him.

They had the name Walter Weldon to give him. Thayer had used it with a new Hartford address when he rented a box.

Nothing of the swashbuckler about him, Madden reflected, with his colorless aliases and thrifty hoarding of ill-gotten money.

He had rented the box October 15, 1959, and visited it with some regularity thereafter. Madden's notebook gave October 14, 1959, as the date of Thayer's first withdrawal from his Johnston account. The amount withdrawn was identical with the amount in one of the envelopes in his brief case. He had made it his practice to withdraw from the Bronx bank one day and visit the Bridgeville bank the next. Only the fifty thousand dollars in the Dunston bank envelope stood out from the rest.

His circumspect comings and goings at the Bridgeville bank had attracted no attention.

The postal inspector promptly phoned this information to Pauling, who had Tad waiting with him at the Medfield police station.

Routine inquiries did the rest. A Connecticut driver's license issued to Walter Weldon, October 8, 1959, gave his new Hartford address. Apparently wary of pushing his luck by using his mailing address on two different driver's licenses, he had taken a room for the month of October 1959 in a Hartford rooming house. The landlady remembered him; he had spent only one night in the room he had paid for a month in advance. He had told her that he was a salesman away most of the time, but she was a veteran landlady and found the one night's occupancy and complete lack of luggage peculiar. She'd been prepared for a woman but there hadn't been one. At the end of the month he had mailed back his key with a note that said he had been transferred and was giving up the room. From the description she gave of him, he had been using his Johnston disguise.

She was more observant than Miss Lazinski. When the inspector showed her several pictures of men wearing glasses, with Thayer's retouched picture among them, she hadn't hesitated over picking him out. "That's the one," she said. "That's Mr. Weldon."

Yesterday in Philadelphia, Pauling's man had located the car rental at one of the larger agencies. Thayer, as Walter Weldon of the Hartford rooming-house address, had rented a black Ford sedan at 7:40 P.M., March 31, and returned it at

5:15 A.M., April 1, driving it 392 miles during the time of use.

Pauling's man, setting out for home, had started from the agency and driven straight to Mrs. Meeker's, recording 195.5 miles for the one-way trip.

But Madden held to the belief that none of this evidence would have broken Thayer. At the very moment of capture it was the loss of the money that had broken him.

When he wasn't talking about it his tone became detached, almost listless, as if he spoke of things done by someone else.

He made no effort to hold back details of the fraud's beginnings. He named the Dunston photographer who had photographed Arthur Williams's picture for him; the Baltimore photographer who had made the composite from it.

In the same detached manner he told of leading Mrs. Meeker to believe that hiring a private detective was her own idea. He had opposed it flatly, he said, making her all the more determined to go ahead with it. Then he let her press him into conceding that he had a friend in the insurance business in Hartford who could probably recommend a good man, but he made a firm issue of it that once he secured the recommendation he was to be left out of the whole business and not have it dumped back in his lap if it didn't work out to suit her. She had agreed to this. The next day he had recommended Henry Johnston to her.

It had gone along just as he had planned it right up until the day she made the fateful call to Hartford.

From the start of the fraud it had become his habit to call her before he came back to Medfield from a trip to make sure nothing had gone wrong in his absence. He had made such a call from Philadelphia, he said, the night he was forced to kill her. Bursting with indignation, she told him about Johnston and that Madden was coming out to discuss the case further with her in the morning. She was in the embarrassing position of being unable to name Thayer's insurance friend;

he had referred to him as Jack and she had forgotten his last name. She said that she hadn't brought Thayer into it yet because she had promised not to dump it back in his lap if it didn't work out; she felt that it wouldn't be fair to tell the inspector that Johnston's recommendation came through Thayer, without talking it over with him first.

It was too bad Mrs. Meeker had been so fair-minded, Madden thought. The cost had been her life.

Thayer had finally calmed her down and got her off her insistence that he come home immediately. He would be there by nine the next morning, he said, get all the facts on Johnston from his insurance friend, and present them to Madden when he arrived.

Mrs. Meeker had been satisfied that it would all be straightened out in the morning.

He would say little about the murder itself. He'd got into the house with a key Mrs. Meeker had once had occasion to give him. He found Mrs. Meeker asleep when he entered her room. He tried to say that there had been no terrible moment of awaking for her, no struggle at all, it had been over so quickly.

Not that quickly, Pauling inserted coldly. She had woke up and she had fought hard enough to kick off the bedclothes.

Thayer made no reply to this.

Madden said, "You took papers from her file on Johnston. You probably left the pictures because you didn't know if Joan Sheldon had ever seen them and you wanted nothing questioned if it was assumed Mrs. Meeker had died a natural death."

"All I took was a Johnston letter that referred to Arthur Williams's foster parents with Cleveland mentioned in it."

"You also took the key to her box in Bridgeport and the paper the Pecks witnessed. You'd talked her into putting fifty thousand aside for some purpose connected with Arthur Williams. Probably it was to go to him if she died before he was found. She must have set some definite time limit on finding him and if it wasn't met, the money was to revert to her estate. No matter how much she trusted you she'd want it in writing with your signature in case you should die too before you could carry out its provisions. The way she handled it was part and parcel of the secretiveness she showed in the whole affair."

Thayer came to life in his hospital bed. That wasn't it at all, he declared. He couldn't remember what the paper was except that it had some bearing on the scholarships; it had nothing to do with the money Mrs. Meeker had told him was to be his when she was gone. She had given him the key to the box.

"She didn't want to leave me anything extra in her will," he said. "She thought the others would resent it and saw no point in causing hard feelings unnecessarily. The arrangement she made was her way of expressing appreciation of all that I'd accomplished with the Meeker Fund."

As he went on protesting his right to the money, Madden had no trouble reading his mind. He had destroyed the paper relating to it. He knew that they had no proof that it was intended for Arthur Williams or that Mrs. Meeker hadn't given him the key to the safe-deposit box. He hoped to salvage this much from the wreckage.

Madden cut short his protests. "It doesn't matter whether you stole the money or she meant you to have it," he said. "Apparently you've forgotten that the law doesn't permit a murderer to profit from his crime."

In his greed for money Thayer, it seemed, had forgotten this. For a few minutes he had been restored to life. Now he lay back on his pillows, drained and defeated again, refusing to say more, demanding his doctor.

They left him white and still, a collapsed puppet whom the doctor at his bedside couldn't hope to reanimate.

Outside the hospital Pauling said, "A heartless bastard, isn't he? He'll get death. And ten years from now when he's used up his last appeal, he'll go to the chair. If they haven't abolished capital punishment by that time."

The inspector laughed at his sour tone. "You should complain. I've got him all wrapped up on the fraud and you take him away from me with your charge of murder."

Pauling had no illusions on what he had contributed. "I wouldn't have got him on the murder at all if you hadn't got him first on the fraud," he said. "That's consolation, isn't it?"

"Not for the leg work I put in at banks," Tad stated.

He didn't mean it. Madden had told him that he would commend him highly for assistance rendered when he made his final report on the case.

It was late afternoon when they got back to the office.

"Anything else scheduled for today?" Tad asked.

"No. You've made plans?"

"Well, I told Joan that if we got back from New London in time and you didn't need me, I'd pick her up for dinner."

"Good idea," Madden approved. "Get Thayer out of your hair. I could do with a dinner date myself. Shall we double?"

"Why—uh——" Tad eyed him in astonishment, rallied from it, and in case Madden was serious said, "Why, yes, I guess we could," but without conviction.

Madden wasn't serious, Tad realized a moment later. He was laughing. "Another time, perhaps," he said.

But he was faintly irked as well as amused. Tad probably thought that any date of Madden's would be a slightly modernized version of Whistler's mother. His jaw would certainly drop if he ever met the attractive redheaded widow Madden meant to ask out to dinner.

In fact, he would make it his business that Tad did meet her before he left Dunston. Whistler's mother, indeed!

The next moment, picking up the phone, Madden began to laugh at himself. Had he actually reached the age where he had to prove to the likes of Tad that there was life in the old boy yet?

During dinner with Joan that evening Tad was thinking, too, of his departure from Dunston in the near future. They had talked briefly about Thayer and now they had turned to the pre-eminently satisfying subject of themselves. Tad mentioned that he would be going back to Washington sometime next week.

Joan looked crestfallen. She had known but lost sight of the fact that his assignment to Madden was a temporary one.

"Where will you be sent when your training period is over?" she asked.

He shrugged. "Only God or the chief inspector could tell you." He spoke lightly but his eyes were serious as he looked at her. "It's nice that we both know how to read and write, isn't it?"

"Well, yes."

"And that the mails I'll be helping to safeguard operate day and night."

She looked happier. "That's right, they do."

His eyes were still serious as he studied her. "You know something," he said gently. "I think I'm in love with you."

"Are you? Well." Joan gave a sigh of deep content. "I hope so. Because I think I'm in love with you."

They had forgotten Brian Thayer's very existence.

He wasn't exactly weighing on Madden's mind, either, at the moment. There were less dreary subjects to talk about with an attractive redheaded widow.